Library and Archives Canada Cataloguing in Publication

Title: Lady Gold investigates : a short read cozy historical 1920s mystery collection / Lee Strauss. Names: Strauss, Lee (Novelist), author.

Description: Short stories. | Content: v. 6. The Case of the Phantom pickpocket -- The Case of the Missing Time traveller.

Identifiers: Canadiana (print) 20190131608 | Canadiana (ebook) 20190131624 | ISBN 9781774092743 (v. 6 :hardcover) | ISBN 9781774092736 (v. 6 : softcover) | ISBN 9781774092767 (v. 6 : IngramSpark softcover) | ISBN 9781774092729 (v. 6 : Kindle) | ISBN 9781774092750 (v. 6 : EPUB) | ISBN: 978-1-77409-504-1 (bookvault)

Classification: LCC PS8637.T739 L34 2019 | DDC C813/.6—dc23

LADY GOLD INVESTIGATES ~ VOLUME 6

A SHORT READ COZY HISTORICAL 1920S MYSTERY COLLECTION

LEE STRAUSS

NORM STRAUSS

THE CASE OF THE PHANTOM PICKPOCKET

1

Ginger Gold, the proprietor of Lady Gold Investigations, and her assistant Magna Jones walked slowly through the jostling throngs of eager shoppers in Petticoat Lane Market. Ginger found a stroll through the market to be an enjoyable break from the sometimes tedious work that came through the office, especially on a delightfully warm spring day.

"Delicious," Magna said, as she took another bite of an apricot that she had bought from a Spanish fruit vendor near the entrance of the market. She wore a knee-length wool skirt and grey cardigan and hat, and dabbed at her chin with a handkerchief to keep any dripping juices from the ripe fruit from damaging her outfit. "I've always loved the satsuma oranges one can buy here in the winter, but these Spanish apricots are scrumptious." Magna raised the fruit into the air as she deftly sidestepped an older man who was distracted by the wares on display and didn't see her coming.

Ginger, in a fitted sweater, an emerald-green pleated skirt and Italian leather boots, pushed a strand of her red bob under her cloche hat as she nodded in agreement, her eyes darting from stall to stall. Beneath strings of flowers hanging like garlands overhead, vendors sold items ranging from freshly baked bread and pies to handmade pottery. "I love this market," she said cheerily, breathing in the heady scents of exotic spices. "A vague sense of unpredictability to keep one on one's toes. Like a microcosm of the city itself, alive and brimming with energy." Glancing at her companion, she added, "Wouldn't you agree?"

Magna, finishing the last of her apricot, nodded as she tossed the pit in a nearby bin. "Absolutely."

Ladies dressed in fine furs and dapper gentlemen in suits and trilbies jostled shoulder to shoulder with working-class families and street urchins. If there was ever a true melting pot of humanity, it was London's sprawling markets. Vendors shouted as they hawked their wares, some of them clanging pots together to get people's attention.

Petticoat Lane Market was of particular interest to Ginger because it was known for its clothing and textile traders, with shops spilling out onto the cobbled street as far as the eye could see. The market was a wonderland of treasures for someone who owned a dress shop like Ginger's own Feathers & Flair. She was always on the lookout for hard-to-find silks from China or original, vibrantly coloured cashmere shawls from India.

Magna paused to examine a tray of gleaming gold jewellery. It was kept under glass at a stall run by an elderly man wearing a white cotton button-up shirt under a black waistcoat. He had leathery skin, a shock of white hair, and kind brown eyes that brightened as he smiled at Ginger and Magna. Next to him stood a younger man, very slim and in his mid-teens, with a strong resemblance to the older man.

Magna pointed to a pair of very large golden hoops that were prominently displayed. "I would look smashing in those earrings, don't you think?"

Ginger raised a thinly plucked brow. "Magna Jones, I have never seen you wear anything remotely like those." The Belgian-born Magna had always dressed plainly and practically. If she wore any jewellery at all, it was in the form of the simplest necklace or bracelet.

"Hmm . . . perhaps you're right," Magna returned. "They might be more suited to you." She pointed to a pair of very ornate bell-shaped earrings. "These are more my style."

"Those are called *jhumka*," Ginger said smiling. "They're very popular in the Far East."

"Yes, very good, madam," the stall owner said. "They'll look very charmin' on you."

"Still a bit extravagant for me," Magna said. "And I do not have anyone I wish to impress. I've given up on men since Rudolph Valentino is no longer alive."

"Valentino!" Ginger remarked with a chuckle. "Yes, I see the attraction. You want someone who can fire a gun, ride a horse, swoop in on an adversary and—"

Magna cut in, "—look good in a trilby *or* a *keffiyeh*. And not just a horseman, Ginger, he needs to be able to command a camel too."

Ginger laughed.

"What?" Magna said, her voice dead serious. "There may be deserts to cross."

"Without a doubt," Ginger said, nodding in mock enthusiasm. "And Bedouin bandits to outrun too."

Magna stared at Ginger with her usual intensely serious expression. "That too."

Ginger found it hard to imagine a man existing who could keep up with the ever-intrepid Magna Jones. She had first met the woman in Belgium during the war. Magna, like Ginger herself, had been working as a spy at the time and had already performed many exploits the likes of which most women would never even dream of.

They stepped to the next stall which featured some beautiful cottons from Egypt.

A bald, olive-skinned man with round wire spectacles and wearing a Jewish *kippa* waved his hand with great flourish over a display of vividly coloured fabrics. "Come and see the beautiful cottons and silks. I have imports from France, Poland and Italy."

His assistant was a slight, dark-haired young woman whom Ginger also pegged to be in her mid-teens. She wore a purple blouse and black pleated skirt along with a pair of attractive 'Jerusalem sandals' made of leather with interlacing straps and a flat heel.

The man noticed Ginger's interest. "This is my daughter, Simcha." The man beamed. "In Hebrew, the word means happiness."

The girl was lovely, but her dark eyes looked

sorrowful, very much the opposite of the meaning of her name.

"You like her outfit?" the man continued. "The fabric for the blouse is very beautiful, yes? It comes originally from Egypt, but I import from a textile house in France."

"It is," Ginger admitted. It was an easy sale for the man, and soon Ginger found herself carrying a bolt of light blue Giza cotton. She didn't know exactly what it would be used for, but she was certain that Emma, her designer, would find some creative use for it.

After meandering amongst the stalls, Ginger was about to suggest to Magna that they work their way back to the office when she was stopped by a sudden shout.

"Stop thief!"

A middle-aged man with expensive-looking cuff-links, a silk tie and leather brogues waved a cane in the air, pointing in the direction where Ginger and Magna were standing. Several people in the market turned to look in that same direction at the same time, and Ginger also turned. However, she saw nothing that indicated any kind of disruption where the man was pointing.

The man shouted, his face red with frustration. "Security! Where is security?"

A man dressed in a blue coat ran to the man. "I'm here. Which way did he go?"

The man pointed again with his cane, and the guard gave chase.

"Did anyone else see the little guttersnipe?" the angry man asked, searching the curious faces around him, but the only response he got in return was a few shrugs and head shakes.

"He would have been an easy mark," Magna said in a low voice to Ginger. "The way he's dressed, the cane . . ."

"This is the third time in the last two days," said the vendor who ran the stall where Ginger had bought the bolt of cotton. He ran over to the aggrieved shopper. "This is the seventh in the last week. On behalf of all the vendors, I would like to express our frustration, kind sir. This is very bad for business for us all. Hopefully the security can catch the little blighter."

Magna's eyes narrowed as her lips pursed. She tapped Ginger's arm. "Perhaps we've found our next case?"

Ginger nodded in agreement. "Perhaps we have."

2

The next day, Mr. John Harris, the owner of the jewellery stall, and Mr. and Mrs Benowitz, who owned the textile stall where Ginger had bought the Giza cotton, presented themselves at the office of Lady Gold Investigations at the agreed-upon time.

Ginger poured the tea. "Thank you, Lady Gold," Mrs. Benowitz said as she and her husband accepted the offering. "It smells most wonderful."

"It's *teh hevrei,*" Ginger said with some pride in her voice. She had made sure to stop at a local shop that morning to buy 'Hebrew tea', a traditional spiced tea enjoyed by many in the Jewish community.

Magna joined them, carrying a tray. "Here's a bit of honey for the tea."

"Oh, and you have Bakewell tarts!" Mr. Harris smiled broadly, his eyes lighting up with delight at the sight of the favorite cake.

Mr. Benowitz put his palms gently together as if in supplication and touched the tip of his nose. "You honour us."

"The pleasure is all ours," Ginger said.

Mrs. Benowitz lifted a teacup to her lips and, almost as if it was a sacred ritual, slowly took a sip, smiled and closed her eyes. Then she lightly put the teacup back down on the side table. Ginger noticed the close resemblance the woman had to her daughter.

"Might I say, Mrs. Benowitz," Ginger began, "your daughter Simcha looked very nice in her outfit yesterday."

"Thank you, Lady Gold. She is to be married soon. There are several celebrations to attend when we get back home to Manchester." She chuckled. "Simcha likes to wear the plain outfits like yesterday, but I have other ideas."

"I find some of the Egyptian fabrics used for everyday wear to be simply fabulous." Ginger sighed. "The fabric of her blouse was quite wonderful."

Out of the corner of her eye, Ginger caught Magna's left knee bouncing up and down like a fidgeting schoolboy. She didn't have a lot of patience when it came to the topic of fashion. Ginger could talk about fabrics and frocks for hours, especially with people from other cultures. However, she took pity on her assistant and changed the subject. To their guests she said, "I assume you have had time to discuss the matter at hand."

"Indeed, madam," Mr. Harris said. "Obviously, we realize that pickpocketing is a normal occurrence in any London market. My workers and I 'ave set up stalls in Croydon market and Spitalfields and also markets in Liverpool and Manchester. There are always reports of sporadic thievery, but in this case they seem to be increasin' to the point of 'avin' an effect on our businesses. Once word gets out, customers will stop comin'."

"This pickpocket has stolen purses, wrist-watches, bracelets . . ." Mr. Benowitz waved a hand in frustration. "The police have not shown much interest in helping us, so we formed a delegation and have hired our own security guards. We can only afford two of them: Mr. Barker and Mr. Stone."

"Petticoat Lane is a large market," Ginger said. "I assume the thief was not caught yesterday."

Mr. Benowitz shook his head. "No. Whoever this pickpocket is, he seems to have a special talent for disappearing."

"Poor Mr. Barker was so out of breath yesterday," Mrs. Benowitz said. "He gave chase through the crowd, but the thief was simply too fast and disappeared in the crowded lane."

"I have given chase myself once," Mr. Benowitz said, "with the help of the person who was robbed. We chased the waif, but he just vanished." For emphasis, he snapped his fingers. "We couldn't believe it."

Mr. Harris nodded with enthusiastic agreement. "My son Lloyd chased him on two different occasions, and even 'is young legs couldn't catch the bloody thief. He said the pickpocket disappeared like a ghost in the night."

"Like a snake in long grass," Mr. Harris added.

Mr. Benowitz hummed. "Like smoke from a tobacco pipe."

"Yes, Mr. Benowitz, that's it!" Mr. Harris slapped his thigh. "Like smoke."

"So you mean to say that people have seen him?" Ginger asked.

"Only glimpses," Mr. Harris replied.

"Can you describe him please?" Magna asked.

"He is young," Mrs. Benowitz said. "Not so tall."

"About thirteen," her husband agreed.

"No more than fifteen," Mrs. Benowitz added. "And thin."

"Like a reed," Mr. Benowitz said.

Mrs. Benowitz nodded. "Like a snake."

"He's like a street cat," Mr. Benowitz said.

"Like a very quick street cat," Mrs. Benowitz agreed.

"All cats are quick," Mr. Harris quipped. He finally gave in to temptation and reached for another Bakewell tart that he had been eyeing.

"Yes, that's true. I have never seen a slow street cat." Mrs. Benowitz, too, reached for a tart. "Even that old one-eyed tabby on our street can move pretty fast when a big lorry comes by."

Mr. Benowitz nodded. "I keep thinking he's going to crash into to the fence or something. He's only got one eye."

Ginger and Magna shared an amused look.

"What about clothing," Ginger asked. "Do you recall what he wore?"

"I caught a glimpse of him yesterday when he stole that man's wallet," Mr. Benowitz said. "He wore a grey cap and grey plimsolls on his feet. His brown jacket was tattered and looked too big for the lad."

"Tattered, ill-fitting clothes, young, thin, fleet of foot," Magna said. "That describes every poor urchin living on the streets of London."

The three stallholders stared back, eyes blinking as they chewed their tarts.

Ginger's mind suddenly went to her adopted son Scout, whom she had taken in a few years earlier. She realized in that moment that her heart might work against her in a case like this. How eager was she to apprehend a child who was probably starving and homeless? London was filled with these "gutter-snipes" as some called them, children with no parents trying to avoid the city's notorious workhouses.

"Well, I don't know if this particular urchin is poor anymore," Mr. Harris said. "Just over the last month 'e must have stolen enough money to rent a nice flat in 'Ampstead."

"Or in Mayfair." Mr. Benowitz took another sip of tea. "I like Mayfair."

Mr. Harris raised his eyebrows and shrugged. "'E could probably buy all of the wares on my stall by now if 'e so chose to. Thank God I keep my jewellery under glass."

"There has been a noticeable decline in wealthier customers coming to Petticoat Lane," Mr. Benowitz said, catching Ginger's eye. "One man, an affluent fellow who comes to my stall regularly to buy imported fineries for his wife, told me that Petticoat Lane is becoming known as the home of the Phantom Pickpocket."

"They've named him?" Magna said with interest.

"Yes," Mr. Harris replied. "Now, we talked to the rest of the stall owners last night at a meetin' after you talked to us. A couple 'ave already 'eard of you, Mrs. Reed. Even though you're a lady, you've earned quite a reputation 'ere in London for bein' a good investigator."

Ginger decided to let the remark about being a woman go by.

"So, you see, we're in a desperate state." Mr. Benowitz leaned forward. "Will you help us?"

3

That evening Ginger and her husband, Chief Inspector Basil Reed, sat beside a crackling fire in the sitting room at Hartigan House. It was their custom to relax there once the residence was quiet, especially after a hard day's work, sipping brandy from crystal glasses. At times they reclined together in comfortable silence, and at others discussed interesting topics of the day.

"Petticoat Lane Market, did you say?" Basil asked.

"Yes. Magna and I have been asked to help catch a thief. He's so elusive they've started calling him the Phantom Pickpocket."

"Really? Well, good luck to you. I understand more constables have been stationed in the vicinity lately but apparently to no avail. They are simply not in the right spot when the robberies happen." He snorted. "Perhaps the moniker is fitting."

"The culprit is likely very young," Ginger said with a grimace. "I imagine he's very much like Scout might've turned out to be had fate not intervened."

As if on cue, a voice came from the doorway. "Mum? Dad? I heard my name. I don't mean to intrude."

Ginger smiled at her fifteen-year-old son and the good manners he exhibited. Long gone was the cockney accent and the less-than-genteel social manners.

"Come in," Basil said. "We were talking about you in a roundabout way."

Scout meandered into the sitting room, his fists stuffed into his trouser pockets. "Did I hear you talking about Petticoat Lane Market?" He flopped into an armchair adjacent to the settee Ginger and Basil occupied, facing the fireplace.

"Are you familiar with it?" Ginger asked.

"Back in the old days," Scout replied with a quick nod, "my mates and I would spend time there, especially towards the end of the day when some of the bakers and fruiterers would sometimes give us handouts before they spoilt."

"Did you and your mates ever steal things from the vendors?" Basil asked.

Scout hesitated.

"It's all right, lad," Basil said with a chuckle. "I'm not about to arrest you for stealing an apple five years ago."

Scout shifted in his seat, averting his gaze to the flames. "One had to be quick about it. Some of those stallholders could run pretty fast."

"What about pickpocketing?" Ginger asked.

Scout grimaced. "Sorry, Mum, but I was pretty good at it. One has to be daring, clever and fast to separate a man from his valuables. Most of the time the mark wouldn't even realize they'd been robbed until later. But sometimes they did, and then the chase would be on."

Basil leaned in. "How did you get away?"

"There are lots of places to hide in the back alleys once you clear the market. Petticoat Lane Market is long but it's also relatively narrow, easy to disappear anywhere around the edges of it."

"How often did you pick a pocket?" Ginger asked.

"Perhaps once a week. More if I spotted an easy mark." Scout ran his fingers through his dark blond hair—very near needing to see a barber, in Ginger's opinion. "Why?" Scout continued. "What's going on?"

"There's been a rash of pickpocketing going on there," Ginger answered. "The stallholders have formed a delegation and hired me to try to find the thief. The descriptions of him are vague. Miss Jones and I are trying to form a plan right now."

Scout's eyes lit up. "I can help!"

"What did you say?" Ginger shook her head in protest. "No."

"Why not?" Scout leaned in, placing his bony elbows on his bony knees. "I know Petticoat Lane like the back of my hand. You know, it's entirely possible that some of my old mates are still there. I might be able to get information that you wouldn't be able to. Perhaps find out who this phantom is."

"It's too dangerous," Ginger insisted.

"How is it dangerous?" Scout challenged. "Has the phantom hurt anyone?"

"Well, no," Ginger admitted.

"And it's my holidays," Scout continued with enthusiasm. "I don't have to go back to school for another week. Let me spend a few hours at the market. You and Miss Jones can be there the whole time, if it makes you feel better."

"An undercover operation," Basil said. "Like a spy."

Ginger started at the mention of the word *spy*. She cast a sideways glance at Basil. "Are you suggesting you're in favour of this plan?"

"I don't see the harm," Basil said, "but this is your case, so it's your call."

"Let me help, Mum. I survived just fine on my own for years in places far more dangerous than Petticoat Lane Market."

Ginger narrowed her eyes as she considered Scout's case. It was true that compared with what his life used to be like, staking out Petticoat Lane Market would be a walk in the park. The plan had merit, but what kind of mother would do such a thing?

"I helped you once before and I can do it again," Scout said. "Don't forget, at one time I was one of those guttersnipes that you are trying to find."

Ginger sighed.

Scout puffed out his chest and pointed both thumbs at his chest. "I reckon I'm the best bloke yer got fer this 'ere job, Mum."

Ginger grimaced inwardly at the sound of the cockney. "Very well." She stared her son in the eye. "But it is a job. I'll pay you like anyone else I employ.

Which means I'm your boss and you have to listen to every word I say and do exactly what I ask of you."

Scout grinned mischievously, suddenly looking very much like the child Ginger had met on the SS *Rosa*. "Yer can count on me, missus."

4

Scout stood at the corner of Wentworth and Middlesex Streets, which marked the beginning of Petticoat Lane Market, and waited impatiently for his mother to finish fussing with his hair.

"If you don't mind me saying so, Lady Gold, your son looks every bit the part of a homeless urchin." Mrs. Benowitz studied Scout with her head cocked to one side and a look of puzzlement on her face.

Scout offered a wide grin. "It's a jolly good thing that the used clothin' stall 'ad me size."

"I wouldn't say your size," Miss Jones returned with a discerning look. "Everything is too big for you."

"That's normal for a street child," Scout

answered. "Either that or too small." He pointed to his feet and added brightly, "Look at these shoes 'ere! They fit me perfect and look just like the old worn plimsolls I used to 'ave, eh, Mum?"

"Indeed." His mum rubbed his right cheek with her handkerchief.

"Mum!"

"I'm just smudging the dirt you rubbed on a bit better."

"Blimey."

His mum shot Scout a look at the use of his language, and Scout stared at the ground. If he was going to be a street urchin, he would have to speak like one, wouldn't he?

"It's odd hearing him speak cockney," Miss Jones said. Scout glanced her way and found her regarding him with a serious expression, like an officer might regard a soldier at inspection time.

"Are you warm enough?" his mum asked. "Those trousers have holes in them."

"Yes, Mum." Scout grinned as he gripped the brim of his woollen flat cap and adjusted it on his head as if tightening a screw.

"All right then, off you go," his mum said with some hesitancy.

"I'll be all right, Mum."

Mum's hand went to her throat. "Miss Jones and I will be walking about within eyesight of Mr. Benowitz's stall. You have two hours to see what you can find. At that time, we will expect to see you at the stall."

Scout knew where he wanted to start his investigation. Just north of Petticoat Lane was an alleyway that led to a small, partially hidden alcove situated behind a Chinese restaurant called The Red Lantern. The place, nicknamed "The Haunt", was a gathering place for the street urchins who happened to be in the area or "working" the market. The small lane was partially covered from the elements and there were even makeshift benches set up along the sides of the lane by the owner of the restaurant, Mr. Chen. He liked to sit out on the back step and smoke a pipe whilst watching games of street football. Sometimes he even brought scraps from leftover meals for the children to share. Scout remembered playing marbles there and had a good collection of "shooters" and "cat's eyes" that he'd won.

It took a few minutes for Scout to find the restaurant again and make his way through a small maze of passageways until he came to The Haunt. Sure enough there was a group of four lads sitting on the benches sharing a cigarette and laughing at some joke, their legs splayed out lazily in front of them. Scout was surprised to feel a slight smile pulling at his mouth. Perhaps not all the memories of his days on the streets were bad.

"What's the John Dory?" Scout said as he approached them. The four lads looked up at once at the newcomer. One was around Scout's age, two about twelve, one a bit younger, at perhaps ten. All were thin and grimy and wearing either a tweed or woollen flat cap.

The eldest held the cigarette. He was lanky and hawkish looking with a long nose and close-set eyes. Scout remembered his face.

The boy looked at Scout with a look of puzzlement as Scout took a seat on a bench across from them.

"Wotcha." Scout touched the brim of his hat in a friendly manner.

"Cor blimey!" A grin spread across the lad's dirty face. "That ain't ol' Scout now, is it?"

"The one an' only," Scout said. Squinting, he added with flair, "Freddie? Is that you, mate? Flippin' 'eck!"

"Stone the crows!" Freddie slapped the leg of the boy next to him. "I knew this snipe when 'e was just no bigger than a squirt!" He gestured with his palm facing the ground to denote someone very short.

"'Ere now," Scout said. "Are yer still 'oggin' all the smokes, then?"

"Ha ha! Yup, that's my mate all right!" Freddie got up and handed the lit cigarette to Scout and stood there for a moment.

"Crikey, where yer been mate?" Freddie said, as he reached out to affectionately shake Scout's hat, and then retake his seat on the bench where the other three boys eyed Scout with interest. "We 'aven't seen you around 'ere for years now. I though yer'd kicked the bucket."

"Never mind that," Scout said. "I want me marbles back." He blew out a plume of smoke.

"Oh my giddy aunt!" Freddie howled, "That's all you got to say now? Where's your bleedin' marbles? You might ask Mr. Chen, he still collects 'em." He pointed his chin at the back door of the restaurant.

"Yup, just jokin'."

"Well blimey, yer just disappeared, din't yer? Yer not at St. Georges, yer not at Croydon market or Billingsgate. Get picked up by a workhouse?"

"Naw, I went on an adventure. Workin' on a ship for a while, mindin' the animals. Spent some time with the circus." Scout thought it best to stick with the truth as much as possible.

"The circus! Good for yer, mate. An' might I say yer lookin' pretty good too. They must 'ave fed yer like a pig at the circus. Are yer back 'ere now, then? We could use a good man like you round here at Petticoat."

"Oh? Why's that? I 'eard you were doin' pretty good all on yer own."

The four lads shared a look.

"What 'ave you 'eard?" the youngest one asked.

"I 'eard that the thievin' 'ere is goin' well. Pick-pocketin' and the like."

"No, it's not goin' well at all." Freddie shook his head sharply. "Yer might 'ave noticed a few more security guards 'ere, and that's not countin' the coppers. There's more o' them too."

"But I 'eard that someone 'as been runnin' off with some good winnin's," Scout said. "It's wot drew me back."

"Yup. Trouble is it's not one of us. An' 'e's doing it way too much. Greedy blighter."

One of the younger boys piped up. "The stall owners 'ave even formed a company o' sorts. Hired a couple of bleedin' guards. Spoils it for the rest of us."

"But 'oo is this bloke, then?" Scout asked.

"None of us know, mate," Freddie said. "But I wouldn't mind givin' 'im a talkin' to." He smashed his right fist into his left palm. "I can tell yer this much though, the bloke's proper good at it! 'E must be, to do it this much and not get nicked."

"'Ave yer ever got a good look at 'im?" Scout asked.

"Nah, he's always gone before any one of us can get 'im in our sights."

Scout emerged from the back alley into the bustling market, fully aware of the suspicious glances he got from some of the stallholders and some of the wealthier marketgoers. It didn't surprise him, but it had been a while since he'd experienced any of that kind of unwanted attention.

He was just about to start heading towards Mr. Benowitz's stall when he noticed a middle-aged woman wearing expensive-looking jewellery and walking with a slight limp. Her handbag dangled loosely from her elbow and was partially open. She seemed to be perpetually distracted by the goods of the stalls as she slowly passed by. Every instinct Scout had ever had as a pickpocket told him that this lady would probably be robbed by the time she left the market. He looked around for a security guard and saw one leaning up against a lamp post, lighting a cigarette. The man had dark brown hair under a grey woollen flat cap and was wearing a black jacket with "Security" emblazoned on it.

Perhaps he should talk to the guard, Scout thought, but by then, it would probably be too late. He could walk with the lady for a while; his presence would likely cause her to be more alert. Or he could hang back and wait for the Phantom Pickpocket to strike. Scout looked up at a nearby clock tower. He had fifteen minutes before he was due back at the Benowitzes' stall.

A street urchin seemed to appear out of nowhere, walking quickly towards the lady. Scout glanced at the guard, but he, rather conveniently, was facing the other direction.

Quickening his step, Scout started towards the lady. The other lad quickened his pace, deftly reached into the lady's handbag, and kept walking in the same direction.

The lady hadn't noticed a thing.

"Stop thief!" Scout shouted as he broke now into a sprint. As he raced past the startled guard, he pointed at the fleeing lad darting artfully through the crowd ahead of him. "C'mon, mister, it's the Phantom!"

Scout struggled to keep the Phantom Pickpocket

in his sights as the thief dodged and weaved through the crowd. It wasn't easy because the lad was short and slight like Scout himself and turned out to be a very agile runner. Scout, who was no slouch when it came to running, had to exert himself to the maximum to keep up.

"Stop!" Scout yelled again. Several people turned to look at the odd sight of a street urchin yelling to stop a thief, but no one bothered to see who he was chasing.

Scout thought he was gaining on the runner when he saw the thief suddenly switch directions and dart down a lane. He remembered that this alley emptied into a dead end where more stalls were set up against a tall brick wall. There was a smaller alley that could be entered from that side street but that, too, was a dead end with no back doors to any of the buildings.

He had him.

Suddenly, a display stand of shoes fell with a loud crash, causing a seafood display and a fruit and vegetable stand to collapse in turn with a kind of domino effect. Scout deftly jumped sideways to avoid being hit by an avalanche of tomatoes. Stall owners shouted, casting blame at one another.

Scout turned back to continue the chase. He had

only lost sight of his prey for a few seconds. After a desperate moment he caught a flash of the thief's grey cap as the lad ducked into the passageway at the end of the market.

Scout sprinted as fast as he could to the end of the street and turned into the dead end. There were two stalls on either side of the alley and two up against the brick wall. Dozens of shoppers were milling about. He quickly found the entrance to the passageway and slowed his pace. He hadn't thought about what to do if he cornered the thief himself. He was winded and he wanted to catch his breath in case there was a struggle. After two turns he came to the brick wall that served as the back exterior of a large hotel. There was no one there.

"Cor blimey!" Breathing hard, he slumped back in defeat against the alleyway wall.

"He just vanished." Scout sat dejectedly on a bench behind Mr. Harris' jewellery stall. "I don't know what happened."

Ginger and Magna stared down at Scout. Ginger, for her part, was very glad to see her son was all right. "Did you get a look at him at all?" she asked.

Scout shrugged. "Skinny. Dirt on his face. Could be any street urchin. When he saw me coming towards him, he took off like a shot. Good leg on 'im."

Ginger frowned at the dropped *H*, but let it go.

"Do you think you'd be able to identify him, if you saw him again?" Magna asked.

Wrinkling his forehead, Scout answered, "I don't know. His cap was pulled down low. His clothes were baggy and worn out." He pulled on his own shirt. "Just like these."

"Not much to go on," Magna said.

Scout stared at the ground dejectedly. "I'm sorry I didn't get him."

Ginger placed a reassuring hand on his shoulder. "You were very brave, Scout."

"Yes, yes, very good lad, very brave," Mr. Harris added, as his white-haired head poked through the dark hanging cloth that separated the space from the front of the stall. "But don't feel too bad. My son Lloyd couldn't catch that little rapscallion either."

"I went to a back alley we used to call The Haunt," Scout said, his face brightening. "A place where the street children hang around. I talked to a couple of lads, including one who remembered me."

"Oh?" Ginger said. She wasn't sure if she should be pleased or concerned.

"His name is Freddie. We used to be mates back in those days. He's not a bad sort really and seems to be doing all right."

"Did they know who this thief is?" Mr. Harris asked.

Scout shook his head. "No, they didn't. They say it's not one of them."

Ginger locked her gaze on her son. "And you believe them?"

"Yes, Mum, I do. If it was one of them, they would be bragging about it. I mean, I'm not saying that stealing is right, but it's how these children survive. If one child happened to steal a wallet or handbag, and there was a lot of money inside, they'd share it."

"If it were one of theirs, they'd know," Magna concluded.

"Yes, Miss Jones," Scout said. "Freddie wasn't too pleased about the Phantom."

"We're dealing with someone who doesn't associate with the usual gang of street urchins in this area," Ginger said.

"I must say, I was surprised at the guard," Scout said, looking puzzled.

Mr. Harris raised a thick, white brow. "Mr. Barker?"

Scout nodded. "At first, he seemed to not notice the lady, even though she was an obvious target for a pickpocket. If I was a guard, I would be focused on watching exactly those types of people, perhaps even approach them and suggest they be more alert. Secondly, it took an awfully long time for him to catch up with the chase. When I started back, he was only just reaching the right turn into the alley."

"Did he seem out of breath?" Magna asked.

"Well, his face was as red as a tomato, and he was gasping a bit and coughin' as well. He had to lean up against a wall for support."

Mr. Harris shrugged. "I would be the same way if I tried to sprint that distance."

Ginger thought the guard looked fit and young enough to make a decent chase. Was he purposefully letting the thief make his escape? She turned to Mr. Harris. "How did you acquire Mr. Barker's services?"

"We took out an advert in the newspaper. 'E was one of the first to answer."

"You said there were two guards," Magna said. "Who is the other?"

"Mr. Stone. 'E answered the same advert."

Magna folded her arms across her chest. "And the two guards work at different ends of the market I presume?"

"Yes, of course."

"Has Mr. Stone ever given chase to the Phantom?" Ginger asked.

Mr. Harris thought for a moment. "You know, I honestly don't know. I would 'ave to ask some of the shop owners with stalls on the other side of the market."

Ginger turned back to Scout. "Did Mr. Barker say anything to you?"

"I asked him if he was going to question the stall owners who were set up in the alley to see if they saw anyone duck into the passageway before I came."

"Good thinking," Ginger said. "What did he say to that?"

Scout scratched his head. "He said he would, and that was the end of our conversation. After that I came right back here."

"Is there anything else?" Magna asked.

"Well . . ." Scout scratched the back of his neck, and Ginger wondered if they'd gone a bit too far dirtying him up. "Just when I thought I was closing in on the thief, a rack of shoes fell over. It distracted me and I lost sight of him."

"A staged distraction, perhaps?" Ginger said.

"A common tactic," Magna said with a quick nod. "I myself have used it." She caught Ginger's eye. "So have you."

"Effective at the right moment," Ginger agreed. "I

believe we may be dealing with not one Phantom, but two."

Scout broke into a wide grin. "I think you're onto something, Mum!"

6

After sending Scout home via the Underground and setting Magna to look for Mr. Stone, Ginger searched for Mr. Barker. It was getting late in the afternoon, and the market would be closing soon for the day, so she hastened her step. She spotted him on the extreme east side of the market near a stall selling spices from China.

"Mr. Barker?" Ginger called out as she approached. "I'm Mrs. Reed from Lady Gold Investigations. I've been hired by the shop owners' delegation. Would you mind giving me a moment of your time?"

The guard's eyes rounded in surprise. "A lady detective? Crikey." He stared past Ginger to the people walking past the stalls.

"I understand that you chased the thief into a back alley today?" Ginger started.

"Yes, I did. 'Ow did yer know that, then?" He looked at her, his eyebrows coming together in puzzlement.

"The young lad who helped give chase is my son. He was in disguise. He took on the job of trying to help find the thief today."

"Well I'll be blowed. You and yer son work together on cases, do yer?" The man lit a cigarette.

"No, not really," Ginger returned quickly, "but in this one, well . . . let's just say he has some special insights for the situation." Turning the focus back to the guard, she asked, "I'm assuming you questioned the stall operators at the end of the alleyway. What did you learn?"

The guard blew a stream of smoke out of the side of his mouth. "None of them saw anythin', but that's not surprisin'. There are lots o' the little criminals runnin' around this market. No reason why they would've taken any special interest in one of 'em, especially if the thief slowed down to a walk when they saw 'im."

"When you were giving chase, were you forced to stop and help with the commotion at the shoe stall near the corner?"

"No, they seemed to be doing awlright. At least no fisticuffs had broken out, so I didn't stop at all. Those kinds of things, with stalls falling over and the like, they seem to 'appen a lot. Those stall owners should give a bit more thought to 'ow 'igh they build their displays, I think. Anyway, I kept runnin'. I'm pretty determined to catch that little guttersnipe, I don't mind sayin'."

"Nothing impeded your progress?" Ginger asked.

"No, I don't recall anything." The man coughed twice, a deep, wet kind of sound coming from deep in his chest, and then took another drag on his cigarette.

"How many times do you think you've given chase to this particular thief?"

"Ha, I've almost lost count now. Probably a dozen times now. The little trickster is really makin' me job 'ell. Every mornin' I pray this will be the day I catch 'im."

"Are you the only one who gives chase?"

"No, there've been times when I didn't 'appen to be there, and one of the stall'olders gave chase, or sometimes the victims, though the thief seems to target those who don't look like they can run very well."

"What about the other guard, Mr. Stone?"

"I don't know. You'll 'ave to ask 'im. 'E and I actually don't 'ave occasion to talk much, an' we make sure we are watchin' over opposite parts of the market."

Ginger paused, then asked, "I understand that you answered an advert to get this job, isn't that right?"

"Yes, madam. But I don't see what that's got to do with anythin'."

"Probably nothing, but it helps me to build an overall picture."

"The stallholders can't blame me that the little waif is so fast and seems to 'ave the knack for disappearin' on the spot."

"No one is casting blame," Ginger said. "These questions are just a matter of form. Now, the requirements for a security guard usually include, among other things, good eyesight, a modicum of physical fitness, basic numeracy and literacy skills, and good references outlining experience in the job. What references did you provide when you answered the advert?"

"I've worked 'ere and there. You know, the usual."

"Mr. Harris mentioned a factory in Cornwall?"

"Yes, Cornwall," the guard returned, vaguely. If one were to pick a county as far away as one could from London without going all the way to Scotland, Ginger mused, it might be Cornwall.

"Mr. Barker, what was the name of the factory you worked in as a security guard in Cornwall?"

"Penpoll." Mr. Barker ground his cigarette out with his heel, looking agitated.

"Is that in Truro?"

"Yes, Truro."

"What do they manufacture at Penpoll?"

"Paper products," he answered gruffly, clenching his jaw. "Again, I don't see the relevance."

"There probably is none," Ginger said. "Are you married?"

"Yes, I am. Now, I don't mean any disrespect, but it feels to me like you're just interested in talkin' about me personal life. As much as I'd like to sit 'ere and 'ave a pleasant conversation with a lady of obvious status, I 'ave other things I need to get to. And seein' as 'ow you're not a copper, an' I'm not under arrest, I'm goin' to be on my way." He touched the brim of his flat cap. "Good day, Mrs. Reed."

7

The next morning, when Ginger arrived at Lady Gold Investigations with Boss in her arms, Magna was already at work at her desk. Without the courtesy of a morning greeting, Magna got straight to business.

"Mr. Stone looks as fit as they come. In his late twenties and very serious looking. When I approached him, he was standing with his arms crossed behind him, legs spread slightly apart like he was head security guard at Wormwood Scrubs! He eyed everyone walking past him like they were all guilty of the worst crimes." She chuckled. "There was never a guard more 'on duty' than Clarence Stone."

Ginger set Boss on the floor and the Boston

terrier headed straight for his basket behind Ginger's desk. "Let me guess," Ginger said as she hung her coat on the rack. "He's never seen the Phantom Pickpocket and has therefore never given chase."

Magna nodded. "Of course, he's heard about the thief, but none of the robberies have taken place near where he patrols. It's a bit odd, isn't it?"

"Indeed. Mr. Barker counted at least twelve times that he has given chase, a number corroborated by Mr. Benowitz and Mr. Harris. There have been more robberies, but those are just the ones where he happened to be near."

"It's surely not happenstance that Mr. Barker was always the guard to give chase," Magna said. "And speaking of giving chase . . ." She stood and struck a mock pose as she ran an arm along the length of her body. "What do you think of my outfit today?" She wore a pair of brown, straight-cut, high-waisted cotton trousers with wide, slightly flared legs. Her high-collared blouse buttoned down the front and fit her loosely. Pointing a toe, she exposed flat, comfortable-looking brogues.

"Definitely ready for action, I'd say," Ginger said with a smile. "Whether that action means shopping or callisthenics."

In response, Magna shot her arms out straight in front of her and started some deep knee bends, blowing air out of her cheeks on every second squat.

Ginger laughed. "The Phantom may meet his match today."

"I was first-place champion in the hundred metre sprint at my school games when I was fourteen." Magna straightened with her hands on her hips. "I also outran two Boche soldiers in the streets of Brussels in 1916." She blew a blast of air out of the side of her mouth, aimed at an errant lock from her dark bob. "They didn't stand a chance."

"The thief usually strikes at least once a day," Ginger said, "and if you shadow Mr. Barker and keep an eye out for likely victims, there's a frightfully good chance you'll get to test out your sprinting skills. There's a possibility that Mr. Barker might be in league with the little thief, so be observant of his actions as well."

"What are you going to do?" Magna asked as she pulled on her spring jacket.

"I'm going to make a telephone call, then head out to visit Mr. Barker's wife. I have the address from his application form that he gave the stall owners' delegation. After that I'll meet you at the market."

Lewis and Nellie Barker lived in a tenement

building in a densely populated working-class area just on the outskirts of east London. Situated near a textile factory, the low rumblings of the large engines that were necessary to run the large looms could be heard in the distance. The front of the building had a communal entrance and Ginger, with Boss on his leash, took the stairs to the third floor. Ginger knocked on the door where the Barkers lived, but after receiving no answer, started making her way back down the hall. Just as she reached the landing, an older woman popped her head out of one of the adjacent flats. Her gaze narrowed as she scanned Ginger from head to toe and frowned when she reached the sight of Boss at Ginger's feet.

"Good morning," Ginger said, cheerily. "I'm looking for Mrs. Barker."

"Across the street," came the gruff reply. "In the allotments. Theirs is number ten."

"Thank you," Ginger said, then headed down the stairs to the ground floor and out the back door where she made her way between the fences that separated the garden plots of the allotments. She found number ten, where in between the rows of vegetables, a woman in her early thirties leaned on a hoe. She wore blue dungarees much like the land girls had during the Great War, her blond hair tied up with a red handkerchief, and she had leather gardening gloves on her hands. She straightened when Ginger approached.

"Good morning," Ginger said. "I'm Ginger Reed from Lady Gold Investigations. Are you Mrs. Barker?"

The woman's gaze immediately fell upon Boss.

"Don't worry," Ginger said. "He's very well trained and won't disturb the soil or the plants. Isn't that right, Boss?"

As if on command, Boss sat down on his haunches and proceeded to look appropriately indifferent.

"A lady investigator with a dog that don't dig." The woman propped a hand on her hip. "All right then, I'm curious."

"I have been hired to investigate a rash of pick-pocketing at the market."

"I've 'eard about the thefts, believe me. My 'usband goes on and on about it. It's 'im that is a guard there, not me, Mrs. Reed. Don't see what you want with me."

"I'm simply doing some background work on all of the guards who work there," Ginger answered reassuringly. "It's normal protocol."

"My Lewis told me you talked to 'im yesterday.

Seems you think he might 'ave something to do with this thievery."

"I didn't say that. I only . . ."

"Lewis Barker would never steal a penny, I can tell you that. In fact, if you want, I can take you up to our 'umble abode across the street and you can search the premises. You won't find any trace of any o' those valuables or any sign of even one extra shillin' in our flat." Her mouth tightened as she dug her hoe into the dirt. "Lord knows we could use it just as much as that bleedin' little guttersnipe 'oo's nickin' from all them rich people."

"I rang the Penpoll factory in Truro this morning," Ginger said softly.

Mrs. Barker's shoulders sagged. Swallowing, she averted her gaze, but said nothing.

"They've no record of your husband working there. You moved here from Cornwall, did you?"

"It's been 'ard for us, Mrs. Reed," Mrs. Barker finally said, her voice betraying a slight tremble. "My 'usband is a good and honest man! He's torn up proper about this thief. He loses sleep over it. If you're going to be the one to make 'im lose his job, just when we really need the money for all those med'cines and that, well then go ahead, let that be on your conscience." She pointed a gloved finger at

Ginger. "But I swear to you as I live and breathe, 'e's got no part in this thievery!"

Ginger raised a brow. "Medicines?"

Mrs. Barker's eyes rounded as she just realized her mistake, then started attacking the soil with her hoe, releasing the unwanted weeds. "I misspoke, Mrs. Reed. Now, if you don't mind, I 'ave a lot of work to do."

8

Ginger dropped Boss off at the office for his midday nap, then met up with Magna at the market as promised.

"*Hawawshi.*" Magna waved a wrap in the air as Ginger approached. "Stuffed with all kinds of delights. This one is beef with onions and Egyptian spices that I can't quite pronounce. Mr. Benowitz recommended it. Delicious."

"You're supposed to be shadowing Mr. Barker," Ginger said with feigned disappointment. "I passed him on my way in."

"The chase is already over," Magna said before taking another bite of the *hawawshi* wrap.

Ginger stared back in surprise. "This early in the day?"

"Our little thief likes to get a head start on things. This time the victim was a man from Glasgow who had a war injury to his left foot. I was reminded this morning that no one can swear like a Scotsman. Except perhaps the Irish."

"Did you catch him?" Ginger asked eagerly. "Has the case been solved?"

"Not entirely."

Ginger ducked her chin. "Not entirely?"

Magna sniffed. "The little rat got away again. I really thought I had him at one point. I was very close."

"Let me guess, something diverted you."

"A workman carrying a ladder stepped right across my path. I didn't get a good look at him, he was partially hidden by the ladder and, of course, he was gone by the time I came back to try to find him."

"What about Mr. Barker?"

"Slow as treacle. And when he finally got to where the chase ended, he was coughing and gasping like an old man."

"I believe he has a medical condition that impedes his athleticism. That doesn't mean he isn't in cahoots with the pickpocket."

"Either that or the Phantom and his gang must

have realized the guard's condition and taken advantage of it."

"They might've seen him chase a previous thief and noticed his lack of stamina," Ginger said, agreeing. "Can you show me where the chase went and where it ended?"

Soon they stood in a passageway that led away from the market to the north, which came to a dead end.

"I caught a glimpse of him going into the alley," Magna said, her voice reverberating off the walls of the narrow space. "Then he was gone. It's almost enough to make me believe in ghosts."

"Can you lift your foot for a moment?" Ginger asked as she crouched close to the ground. "The right one will do."

Magna shot her a questioning look. "What?"

"Your right foot," Ginger repeated. "Step a little closer please."

Magna leaned on the passageway's brick wall for support as she lifted the bottom of her shoe for Ginger to inspect.

Ginger pointed to an imprint in the dirt. "This footprint is yours." Motioning to the greater area she added, "This passageway seems to be muddier than some of the others. You see how no one has been in here since the last rain except for you and one other person?" She moved closer to a second, smaller print.

"Ah, not a ghost," Magna said, "Looks like a pair of worn plimsolls."

"You can see by the collection of prints that the thief shuffled around a bit, and then he must have left again."

"No doubt covered in invisible paint," Magna said haughtily, "because I didn't see him, and he would've had to pass me to get out. "

Ginger bent down again to inspect one of the prints which was comparatively well defined. "This is odd."

"What is it?" Magna asked.

"This print is different from the rest. Look, there's a few more over there. There's none of this type coming in that I can see, but there are going out." Ginger straightened, catching Magna's eye. "We need to ring the police and get an officer to make a plaster cast of this footprint. I think it's preserved well enough to do that."

Magna squinted. "But isn't there any number of street boys that would match those prints?"

"This shoe has a slightly more defined arch and narrower heel than most," Ginger said. "It compares to yours in that way, only this person is smaller and lighter than you. The tread is also quite unusual and very clear. In other words, the tread is not worn very much. It's a newer shoe, or possibly a sandal of some kind."

"So . . ." Magna returned.

Ginger cocked her head. "This might be a woman's footprint."

"Ah," Magna said with a slow nod. "The baggy clothes. One can hide a skirt under a baggy shirt."

"It would only take a moment to pull a skirt out from under a big shirt and cover a pair of trousers that had been rolled up," Ginger said. "Hide a cap under the arm, change from your worn plimsolls into women's footwear of some kind. She could have had them tied around her waist, under her shirt."

"A lad enters the alley and poof, like a magic trick, a girl emerges." Magna grinned. "I have to admire that."

"And not just any girl," Ginger said as she started out of the alley. "One very special girl."

THE NEXT MORNING, Ginger and Magna approached Mr. Benowitz's stall and invited him to join them behind it.

"What is in this interesting-looking suitcase?" Mr. Benowitz asked.

Ginger placed the metal case on the wooden table, unlocked the latch and opened the lid. "This was made yesterday by the police. It is a mould of the thief's shoe."

Mr. Benowitz scratched his chin. "How do you know it belonged to the thief?"

"Because Miss Jones gave chase and hers were the only other prints at the scene, before the thief got away."

"Aha, I see," Mr. Benowitz said agreeably. "How do they make it?"

"They first brush the surface of the footprint with a fine powder, like talcum," Ginger said. "Then they just pour plaster of Paris on it and allow it to harden. It only takes thirty minutes or so."

"So now we try to find the shoe that matches," Mr. Benowitz said. "This is very clever. It's like that French folk story of the girl with the little glass slipper."

"*Cendrillon*," Magna said with a nod. "Or in English, Cinderella."

"But what do we do now?" Mr. Benowitz's eyes squinted with a look of helplessness. "Round up all the street urchins in the area and check if one of their shoes matches? And I can't imagine them cooperating."

"If I'm right, I don't think we'll need to do that." Ginger looked carefully at the stall keeper. "You'll notice the arch is deep, the heel smaller, with a unique design, different from most British-made shoes."

They were interrupted by a soft voice. "*Abba*? We are getting very low on the mulberry silks." Mr. Benowitz's daughter poked her head in, her black hair tied back and off her face. "Shall I fetch some more?"

"It can wait until later, Simcha," Mr. Benowitz said. "I can go and get some myself."

Simcha's round eyes settled on the plaster-cast print sitting on the table.

"What's that?" she asked warily.

"It's rather interesting, Simcha," Mr. Benowitz said. "It's a cast of a footprint belonging to the Phantom Pickpocket, and now we must—"

A small cry escaped from Simcha's mouth before she disappeared in a flash.

"Simcha!" Mr. Benowitz shouted. "What's the matter, daughter? Come back here!"

Ginger shot a look at Magna. "Let's go!"

They ran around the stall just in time to see

Simcha's slim figure feint to the left and then dart to the right as she deftly manoeuvred around the outstretched arms of Mr. Stone who had been waiting for her in front of the stall as instructed.

"Cor blimey," the man said as he spun around, one hand holding his cap in place.

"The chase is on!" Magna yelled as she, Ginger, and Mr. Stone joined in pursuit.

Ginger hadn't sprinted much at all since the birth of her daughter, Rosa. She was glad that at Magna's suggestion, she had joined in for some callisthenics before leaving the office in anticipation of the morning's possible events. Even so, she could now feel her calves begin to burn.

With Mr. Stone in the lead, they raced through the streets, weaving and sidestepping, trying to at least keep the tall security guard in view. He presumably had the fleeing form of Simcha Benowitz in his sight, ponytail flailing behind her. Fortunately, the market was still reasonably empty at this time of morning, ensuring mishaps with east London shoppers were kept to a minimum.

Up ahead, Ginger saw Mr. Stone frantically gesture with both hands that Ginger should go down one street, while Magna went down the other.

"I will go ahead!" he shouted. "The three lanes meet up at the end."

Ginger understood the idea was to seize the girl before she could find a way out of the market.

Trying to keep her breathing steady, Ginger raced down the lane that veered to the right, trying to get to the end as soon as possible.

As the lane started curving to the left, she caught sight of a slender figure exiting into an alleyway on the right. Ahead she saw Mr. Stone with Magna follow the girl into the alley.

Ginger finally emerged into a dead-end passageway. In addition to four very surprised-looking young lads who were in the middle of a game of marbles were Magna Jones and Mr. Stone, the latter looking rather red in the face. Simcha Benowitz, the object of their chase, sat on a bench with her face in her hands, weeping bitterly. Beside her, with his arm protectively around her shoulders, his dark eyes full of anger as he stared up at her pursuers, was Lloyd Harris, son of Mr Harris.

9

*S*itting around a table in a Scotland Yard interview room were Mr. Harris, his son Lloyd, Mr. and Mrs. Benowitz and Simcha Benowitz, who sobbed quietly while sitting next to her mother.

Though common thievery wasn't Basil's department, Ginger had asked him to take the lead. Her husband was the only one who'd allow her to be part of the interview.

Ginger and Basil took the remaining empty chairs, and Basil began, "As I understand it, Miss Simcha Benowitz and Mr. Lloyd Harris here operated a scheme to steal from customers at Petticoat Lane Market. Mr. Harris provided the distractions needed for Miss Benowitz to elude capture. Is this correct?"

"Yes, sir," Simcha said with a shaky voice between sobs. "That is correct."

"And you've surrendered all the valuables as evidence."

"Of course she has!" Mr. Benowitz burst out, the veins on his forehead bulging. "None of it has been sold."

"Thank you, Mr. Benowitz," Basil said, "but I would like to hear it from your daughter."

Keeping her gaze averted, Simcha confirmed her father's statement. "I didn't sell any of it."

"The coalition of stall owners for Petticoat Lane have agreed to take out an advert in the most important London newspapers, and, with the help of the police, hope to find the rightful owners of the valuables as soon as possible," Mr. Harris added quickly.

Mrs. Benowitz nodded her affirmation as she wiped her own eyes with a handkerchief. "This is so . . ." She swallowed hard, unable to finish her sentence.

"Miss Benowitz," Ginger started, speaking gently to the daughter. "It's easy to understand the motive for a young street urchin with no home or support to be driven to thievery, but you have a loving, caring family. What drove *you* to do these things?"

"Yes, I have been wondering the same thing!" Mr.

Benowitz said, his dark eyes flashing with a storm of mixed emotions. "You're a good girl. You have been your whole life." He rubbed his hand over his mouth and then shrugged helplessly. "Your mother begged me not to bring you to London. We could have left you at home with your aunts and cousins. Perhaps she was right."

All eyes focused on Simcha Benowitz, the Phantom Pickpocket.

"I . . . was planning on running away," she said finally, her voice barely above a whisper. "I'm a woman. I don't have my own money, and I needed some."

"Why? What on earth?" Mr. Benowitz couldn't conceal his bewilderment. "Have we mistreated you, Simcha? You know how much I adore you. You are my moon. Never has a daughter been more prized by her father than you."

For the first time, Simcha looked her father in the eye. "I know you and mother love me but . . ." She glanced at her mother, including her. "But you never listen to me. I don't want to marry Isaac Schwartz!" Her voice cracked and her eyes glistened with fresh tears. "I would rather die!"

"But Simcha!" Mrs Benowitz protested. "It's a

good match. His family is very prominent in Manchester and he's a good man!"

"He's forty years old. An *old man*! And I don't care about his family name."

"What would you rather do then?" Mr. Benowitz shot an angry glance at Lloyd Harris. "Marry *this* lad?"

"There is nothing wrong with my son!" Mr. Harris' voice pitched higher with indignation.

Lloyd looked like an animal caught in a snare, with wide, frightened eyes, his slender frame trembling.

"Lloyd was helping me to escape a dreadful situation," Simcha said. She stared at the young man as a tear ran down her cheek. "He's a good friend."

"Very well," Basil said. "We're not here to settle family matters. Now that we understand the motive, I'd like to hear you describe how you did it."

"I had a simple disguise at the ready," Simcha said, drying her eyes. "I carried my sandals tied around my waist along with my skirt under my baggy shirt as I ran. When it came time, it only took a moment to roll up my trousers under my skirt and slip on my sandals. No one noticed that I still had the same shirt on. The cap was also easy to hide under there." She paused then added, "I kept my eye out for shoppers who looked well-to-do, who were a bit sloppy with their possessions, and whom I felt I could outrun."

"I would create a diversion, if needed," Lloyd said. "We had prescribed routes that she would run, always in Mr. Barker's section." He glanced up apologetically. "He's not a very fast runner."

Later at the office of Lady Gold Investigations, Ginger recounted the interview to Magna.

"Simcha Benowitz has to appear before a magistrate in court," Ginger said. "Given this is a first offence and that she has family support, there's a chance the judge might be lenient."

"I do hope so," Magna said. "I have to admire the girl's pluck."

"And her resourcefulness."

"Not to mention her fleetness of foot."

Ginger nodded her agreement. "In another time and place, she would've been recruited into the Crown's service."

Magna worked her lips. "That kind of service is ongoing. Perhaps we should put forth a recommendation."

"To whom?" Ginger asked suspiciously.

Magna grinned slyly. "I have connections."

Ginger didn't doubt it, as she had a few of her

own as well. "Miss Benowitz is only seventeen," she said. "Let's give her a bit more time."

"Of course," Magna said with a flick of her hand. "But if I hear of another unhappy arranged marriage—"

"Let's cross that bridge if or when we come to it, shall we?" Leaning back in her chair, Ginger tapped her fingertips together. "Now, do we have another case?"

THE CASE OF THE MISSING TIME TRAVELLER

1

Ginger and Scout stood in front of the entrance to the Grand Hall at Olympia in Kensington and stared up at the huge brick archway.

"Crikey," Scout said in a whisper as he stood there with his hands at his sides.

It was indeed an impressive sight. The archway was flanked by tall pillars and decorated with ornate carvings and sculptures depicting Greek mythology. A massive banner above the decorative double metal doors read "International Inventions and Innovations Exhibition" in bold lettering.

"I think you'll enjoy this," Ginger said as they entered the Grand Hall with its vast glass dome. Exhibits filled the cavernous space, showcasing the latest in engineering and scientific innovations. The sound of machines whirring, steam hissing, and visitors excitedly chattering created an enticing sensory experience. The air was alive with new possibilities.

Every booth had some kind of display featuring something new and bold. Ginger and Scout paused in front of an exhibit called "General Electric Monitor Top Refrigeration," where a white-enamelled metal cabinet was on display. It stood five feet high and had an apparatus on top which resembled the turret of a battleship. A man dressed in a pinstriped suit, who stood in front of a flip chart showing various diagrams, spoke to a small crowd made up mostly of women.

He opened up the front of the refrigerator to reveal wire shelves and compartments for storing food. "This beauty is the absolute latest and best in refrigeration design. The enamel finish makes it easy to clean. There's even a tray where one can put water and slide it into a compartment to make ice." This elicited oohs and aahs from the small crowd. "It works by circulating a coolant through a series of coils located on the back of the cabinet."

Ginger, always impressed by new technology, said, "I bet Mrs. Beasley would love this new contraption."

After buying Scout a small tin of peanuts at a kiosk, they moved through more exhibits of exciting new household gadgets, including an electric washing machine and an electric iron. "Lizzie would appreciate that," Scout said. "No need to heat it in the stove first."

A man running a booth displaying an automatic toaster boasted, "You have never seen such an evenly toasted piece of bread. No need for an open flame, and it pops up when finished!"

The larger exhibitions featured new innovations in transport, such as better steam engine components and sleek new automobile designs.

"Look, Scout, this one is showing how cars are now being made with those new hydraulic brake systems, and they are fitted on all four wheels."

Ginger had more interest in mechanics than most women, which had been a necessity during the war years.

"What does hydraulic mean?" Scout asked as he stared at one particularly unusual-looking car with its deep blue paint sparkling under a set of spotlights.

"Well, it's written here on this board," Ginger said.

Scout read aloud, "A special type of fluid is

forced through a system of pipes when one depresses the brake pedal. This fluid transmits pressure to brake pads made of asbestos that then transmit and exert that force onto the wheels." He grinned at Ginger. "What will they think of next?"

They made their way to a series of exhibits in a section called "Technology of the Future." Presented were speculative inventions in development, including those found in the minds of science fiction aficionados, things like perpetual motion machines and different types of flying cars. There was even a radio spectroscope, a device meant to pick up radio signals from distant galaxies. Some hoped to be able to use it to prove that there was life on other planets.

"Look, Mum!" Scout pointed at an exhibit called "A Time Machine".

A man with unruly grey hair and wild-looking eyes and wearing a white lab coat stood in front of a dummy dressed in an odd-looking suit. Behind the suit was a large blackboard with schematics drawn on it.

"Travelling through time is entirely possible, ladies and gentlemen," the man said with a measure of intensity, addressing the spectators in front of him. "One just has to have the correct quantum calculations and a proper suit made out of the right materials." He gestured to the dummy. "I propose an apparatus like the one you see before you."

The sturdy-looking brown leather suit had a collection of straps and buckles and was reinforced with brass grommets. Heavy-looking black rubber boots were permanently attached to the legs and looked entirely weatherproof. The dome-shaped helmet was fashioned from a smooth metallic material with a series of lenses and dials attached to the exterior. A large circular lens took up the face of the helmet, which was framed by smaller lenses and other mysterious-looking instruments. Hoses and cables ran into a steel compartment, like a boxy knapsack, on the back of the suit.

The man continued, "The inner workings of the box on the back are an amalgamation of rare and exotic metals, each with its own unique properties." The odd man waved a pointer. "The suit is outfitted with an intricate network of gears, levers, and switches which work in concert to power the temporal mechanisms within. At the heart of it is a type of engine I call a 'Quantum Chrono-Displacer'. It is fuelled by a rare mineral, the existence of which has hitherto only been theorized, known as Kronium."

This was met with mild laughter from several people in the crowd.

A man shouted, "Have you been to visit the Pharaohs yet?"

"Perhaps you can go to the future and get some information for that man in the flying car exhibit," said another, with a laugh. "You could help him get off the ground, so to speak."

More derisive laughter rose from the crowd, as the onlookers started to disperse.

The inventor set his pointer on a table and shook his head, his eyes filled with disappointment.

Much to Ginger's surprise, Scout had left her side and walked directly up to the inventor. "Will it really work, sir?"

The man regarded both Scout and Ginger with an intensely curious expression, as if he'd never seen a lady with red hair, or a lad with a tin of peanuts before.

"Professor Willington, at your service," he offered with a slight bow. "Young man, what do you know about the quantization of energy as described by Max Planck and others?"

Scout's eyebrows squished together. "The quanti ... what?"

"Schrödinger described it quite well by calling

it the mechanics of quantum or *quantum mechanics,* that is to say the study of things very small, so small they can't be seen by the naked eye." The professor gazed off into the distance as if suddenly receiving a vision along a mysterious horizon. Slowly he turned back to Scout as the vision dissipated. "Did you by any chance go to the Solvay Conference in Brussels last year? I don't think I saw you there."

Scout stared questioningly at Ginger.

"I'm afraid a trip to Brussels wasn't part of his school lesson planning," Ginger said.

"Oh, I see." The professor tapped his fingers on his chin, "So you don't know about wave-particle duality, then?"

Scout shook his head helplessly.

"No matter, no matter." Professor Willington looked into Scout's eyes as if searching for something. "Ah yes, I see it. There's some spark there all right. You're a good lad, aren't you?" The professor straightened. "If I sent you back in time to . . . let's say the Renaissance, you wouldn't muck things up, would you?" The professor's expression was frightfully grave, and Ginger believed the man was asking the question in all sincerity.

"I hope not, sir," Scout said.

"You wouldn't try to overthrow Henry the Eighth or anything like that?"

"No, not at all."

"You wouldn't write down Romeo and Juliet just before Shakespeare did, and then claim you wrote it?"

"I wouldn't, sir," Scout said. "I don't know Romeo and Juliet, but all the same, I wouldn't."

"And if you went back to the time of the caveman you wouldn't try to give him a box of matches, would you? Because that would really muck things up."

Ginger's hand flew to her mouth in an effort to suppress a giggle. The professor was quite a character!

"I might take a box of matches with me so I could start a warm fire at night to help me survive such a trip," Scout said, "but I would be careful not to let the caveman see it."

"Now, there's a good lad!" Professor Willington ran a hand through his hair, making it stand on end even more. "One more thing. Above all, young man, and this is very important . . . under no circumstances are you allowed to go back in time, fall in love, and attempt to bring that young lady back to 1928 with you! Is that understood?"

"Stone the crows!" Scout protested. "I'm too young to fall in love."

"I loved a girl when I was your age," the professor returned seriously. "It can happen."

He turned back to the board and madly started drawing diagrams. "Now, in order to travel through time, we must find a way to manipulate the fabric of space–time itself. This can be accomplished through the use of my Quantum Chrono-Displacer, which is capable of generating a field of temporal energy that can distort the fabric of space–time."

"And this device is fuelled by Kronium?" Scout ventured.

"Marvellous!" Professor Willington spun on his heels, his eyes bright with appreciation. "You've paid attention. I recently confirmed that this rare mineral exists in Algeria. I plan to get my hands on it." The professor threw up his hand in front of him to make the point, thereby losing his grip on the chalk, which flew high into the air and dropped at Ginger's feet.

"Oh, I'm terribly sorry, madam," the professor said as Ginger handed it back with a polite nod. He then turned back to the board and started drawing all manner of circles, angles, mathematical equations and indecipherable scribbles. On several occasions, he paused to point his chalk at Scout who stood open-mouthed beside Ginger.

"When the Quantum Chrono-Displacer is activated, it creates a localized temporal distortion that allows an object or person to enter into a parallel temporal dimension. This parallel dimension is essentially a separate version of space–time that exists in a different point in time. The Quantum Chrono-Displacer navigates through this parallel dimension, using a complex algorithmic process to calculate the optimal path through the temporal landscape. This process involves analysing various temporal variables, such as the mass and energy of nearby objects, the curvature of space–time, and the rate of time dilation." He stopped speaking for a moment while his chalk scribbled violently on the board.

Ginger shared a look with Scout who shrugged. She was ready to move on, but Scout seemed rather taken with the old professor, and it would've been rude to walk away in the middle of his explanation.

"Once the optimal path has been calculated," Professor Willington continued, "the Chrono-Displacer generates a high-energy temporal vortex that allows the traveller to enter into the desired point in time. The temporal vortex connects the traveller's current location in space–time to the desired point in time, allowing them to traverse the temporal landscape with incredible speed."

He tapped his chalk on the board dramatically to mark a period at the end of a sentence, and then stepped back from the board with his hands on his hips, surveying his work. "That's all of it. This shows how it works and why."

The board was now filled with diagrams of connecting circles and curved lines and long mathematical sequences with equations whose meaning Ginger couldn't even guess at.

Catching Scout's eye, Ginger asked teasingly, "Did you get all that?"

Scout stood with his mouth open for a moment before answering, "I might need to study it a bit more."

"You just strap yourself in, adjust those dials there and say your prayers." Professor Willington pointed to his suit-like contraption. "You could bring a packed lunch if you liked. I suggest an egg sandwich."

"May we take a photograph, sir? It would help me if I could study it."

"Very well, young man! But I will ask you not to show the picture to anyone." The professor narrowed his eyes, his bushy eyebrows meeting in the middle as if they were one. "There are unscrupulous characters who would love to get their hands on these calculations." He then abruptly straightened up and looked warily around at the other exhibits before rushing to the board, one hand gripping the eraser, the other using his lab coat sleeve, to frantically wipe his work off the board. Ginger barely snapped the photograph in time.

"Remember this," Professor Willington said as he finished wiping down the board, "you should attempt only to go *back* in time. Not forward. It's far too dangerous."

The poor man was suffering from paranoia.

"More dangerous than going to the past?" Scout asked. "Why would that be?"

"Well, because the future hasn't happened yet." The professor shrugged as if this was glaringly obvious.

"Have you gone back in time yet?" Scout asked.

"No, as I said, I have only recently confirmed the existence of Kronium. I plan to launch the maiden voyage of the suit after I get back from Africa." He brought his face closer to Scout's and dropped his voice to a whisper. "Only by attempting the absurd can a man achieve the impossible."

2

Two weeks later, Ginger and Magna Jones, Ginger's intrepid assistant, were enjoying their customary morning tea together in the office of Lady Gold Investigations when Ginger's eyes fell upon an article in *The London Times*. She sat forward immediately at her desk, her mouth dropping open.

"What is it?" Magna asked.

"He told us it was too dangerous."

"Too dangerous?" Magna's eyes rounded in interest. "Who? What?"

"Professor Willington, an inventor Scout and I met at the International Inventions and Innovations Exhibition. He said it was too dangerous to attempt to go *forward* in time." Ginger handed the paper over to Magna. "He told us one should only go back in time."

"I think I should like to stay right here in 1928!" Magna declared as she took the paper from Ginger.

London, 24th August 1928 - In a bizarre incident, a man who claimed to have invented a time travel machine has vanished without a trace during a test run in his home. The inventor, Professor Edward Willington, had been working on his invention for several years and had finally built a machine that he believed could transport individuals through time.

Professor Willington left a note saying that he would set the dials to travel one hundred years into the future to the year 2028. Witnesses report seeing a bright flash of light emanating from his window. Fearing an electrical fire or explosion, when no one answered the door, they alerted the authorities.

A search party was immediately dispatched to Professor Willington's home, but there was no sign of the inventor or his time travel suit. The police have launched a full investigation into the incident and have not ruled out foul play.

Professor Willington's claims of inventing a time travel suit had been met with scepticism by the scien-

tific community, who dismissed it as a mere fantasy. However, the disappearance of Professor Willington has reignited the debate about the possibility of time travel.

There have been some speculations that Professor Willington's invention may have been a success, and that he may have travelled through time but has been unable to return to the present day. Others have suggested that the suit may have malfunctioned, causing the inventor to be transported to another time period or dimension than intended.

Despite the mystery surrounding the incident, the police have appealed to the public for any information that could lead to the discovery of Professor Willington's whereabouts. The search for the inventor and his time travel suit continues, as the world waits with bated breath for any new developments in this strange and fascinating case.

"Ginger, you don't actually believe that this man has managed to invent time travel, do you?" Magna slapped the paper onto the desk. "This article reads like an H.G. Wells novel."

"No, I don't, but Scout was quite taken with him. He will be very excited to read this article. One might almost begin to think that the professor's anticipated maiden journey was at least partially successful."

Magna scoffed. "Successful?"

"You'll have to admit, it's an intriguing mystery at least," Ginger said.

"It's fanciful thinking to believe one can travel through time," Magna said.

"I don't disagree, but," Ginger lowered her voice, "I *will* tell you a secret that most people don't know."

Magna looked once around the room and then lowered her voice, too, as she leaned forward. "What's that?"

"Only by attempting the absurd can a man achieve the impossible."

"Or a woman," Magna said without missing a beat.

"Or a woman," Ginger agreed.

Just then, the chime over the front door rang and a middle-aged woman wearing a plain brown jacket and hat stepped timidly into the room "Excuse me. Am I in the right place?"

"This is Lady Gold Investigations," Ginger said. The woman must have habitually walked with her head down to have missed the sign situated clearly above the door. "Is this the enterprise you're looking for?"

"Oh yes, please. I'm so sorry to disturb you. I'm Mrs. Rawlings and I would like to enquire about your services. Do you have a few minutes for us to talk, or do I need to make an appointment?"

"As it turns out," Ginger said with a smile, "we're available now. I'm Mrs. Reed, also known as Lady Gold, and this is my assistant Miss Jones." Ginger waved to an empty leather-padded chair. "Please have a seat. Now, how can we help you?"

Mrs. Rawlings managed to lift her gaze to meet Ginger's eyes. "My employer is missing."

"And who is your employer?" Magna asked, pencil and paper at the ready.

"Professor Edward Willington."

Ginger and Magna shared a surprised look.

"Miss Jones and I were just reading about his disappearance," Ginger said. "Is he still missing?"

"Yes, madam, and I'm becoming very concerned, I don't mind saying. I'm his housekeeper. And well, not to be blunt, but without him, I'm out of a job."

"I understand that the police are looking into it," Magna said.

Mrs. Rawlings held tightly onto her handbag on her lap. "Not really. Apparently, they want to wait a while to find out if he's really missing at all. Perhaps he's just gone on holiday or something, they say."

"I presume Professor Willington is unmarried," Ginger prompted. "Or perhaps he's widowed?"

"He's not a widower, madam," Mrs. Rawlings said. "Married to his work, he says. Though he did mention, a long time ago now, mind you, something about a young lady that he fell in love with as a youth. I think he said she lives somewhere in Ireland, which could explain why the romance was doomed." She shrugged, then added, "I've been working for Professor Willington for over fifteen years, you know. He lives out in Uxbridge in a place called Fernleigh House. I don't live in, but I come most days to look after him. I do the dusting and the cleaning and some of the cooking, and there's a local woman who comes twice a week to do the heavy work. I also feed the cat. The professor is very fond of that cat. Calls her 'Miss Fluffington'." Mrs. Rawlings smoothed the wrinkles on her skirt. "The professor isn't exactly a tidy man, if you know what I mean, so it's a bit of a job. Certainly he's eccentric, but he's also very kind and generous. He pays me a nice wage and gives me birthday and Christmas bonuses."

"Are there other staff?" Ginger asked.

"Just old Mr. Banner who does the gardening."

"Was it you who called the police?" Magna asked.

"No, it was the milkman, Rush, who saw the light flash. He'd just delivered the milk to the kitchen door and was about to drive away when he saw the bright flash coming from the second-floor window." She nodded knowingly. "The professor's laboratory is there. Apparently, it was as bright as the sun for a second, looked like a flash of lightning. When Rush shouted up at the window and got no reply he got concerned and ran inside to have a look around. When the professor couldn't be found, Rush summoned the police. They did a search but didn't find the professor or the time travel suit."

Mrs. Rawlings reached into her handbag, removed an envelope and placed it on Ginger's desk. *For Mrs. Rawlings* was the only thing written on the front.

"I found this through the letterbox at Fernleigh House the day after the professor disappeared," Mrs. Rawlings said. "There's no postage on it, so I figured it must've been delivered by hand."

Ginger opened the envelope and pulled out the letter. The handwriting was barely legible, but Ginger immediately recognized the same wild, scribbling style that was displayed on the professor's chalkboard at the exhibit.

My Dear Mrs. Rawlings, I am writing this in anticipation of certain events occurring. If you read this it means that I am not around to cancel its delivery. Please don't worry about me. I'm all right, I'm sure. I made sandwiches with some of your excellent homemade jam and I've brought a tin of biscuits in case I am gone for longer than I expect. I only hope they still drink tea in the far future.

As you are no doubt already aware, I have set the dials on the suit for the year 2028. There is no particular reason for that year specifically, only that it represents 100 years into the future, which I find a nice round number.

I hope I make it back, but it is possible that I may be stuck there for a while. I took my satchel with me with all my notes because I don't want it to fall into the wrong hands. There are unscrupulous parties who have been after my work for some time, and I don't want to give them the opportunity to steal it while I'm gone.

If I make it back, and all goes well, there will be significant ramifications, the likes of which have never been witnessed since the world began. I feel like I am on the brink of seeing the course of human history and our role in the cosmos being altered forever. If I don't make it back within a year, I've arranged with my solicitor to provide for you.

Destiny awaits!

Yours,

Professor Edward Willington

P.S. Please don't forget to feed Miss Fluffington.

Ginger lowered the paper.

"Forgive me, Mrs. Reed," Mrs. Rawlings said, "I don't believe in time travel, or any of that fanciful stuff, but I do believe there are those with black hearts who want Professor Willington's notes. He's a very brilliant man, you see."

Ginger passed the letter to Magna, then turned to their new client. "Mrs. Rawlings, can you give me a list of people that you have seen at Fernleigh House in the last month?"

3

rofessor Rupert Moody was one of the foremost instructors that the Kelvin Institute of Engineering and Design in Walton-on-Thames had ever had during its 200-year history. Ginger knew this to be true because it was one of the first things the man told her when she met him in his classroom after all the students had left.

In his early sixties, with heavy jowls and greying hair and beard, Professor Moody leaned up against the wooden lectern used when teaching. "The Kelvin Institute may be only a small technical institution, but it's a good one. The Moody family goes back generations in the field of inventions, and quite a few notable inventors were educated here. My grandfather William Rupert Moody invented the

'Moody Gauge', a pressure sensor used for the mass production of a type of railway system that would run on compressed air."

"How frightfully impressive," Ginger said. "I've never heard of such a thing."

"Yes, well, the whole idea of that railway system never came to fruition," the professor admitted. "It was deemed too dangerous." He cleared his throat. "I'm currently working on a new prototype myself."

"I see. Well, good luck with that," Ginger said sincerely.

"What can I help you with today, Mrs. Reed? You said you are a private investigator, didn't you?"

"Yes, I have been engaged to look into the disappearance of Professor Willington."

"Ah." Professor Moody nodded sombrely. "I read the story in the newspapers. I'm not sure what that has to do with me though."

"His housekeeper says you were at Fernleigh House two days before he disappeared."

"Indeed, I was. Willington had just returned from Africa a few days earlier. He wanted to show me the newest prototype of that blasted suit."

"You don't appear to be impressed with his invention," Ginger said.

"Willington is a brilliant man, Mrs. Reed, don't

get me wrong, but he isn't . . ." Professor Moody's eyes rolled upwards. "Not to sound unkind, but I don't think he is in full control of his faculties."

"Yet you went to see the time travel suit."

"Naturally! I'm curious by nature. If I believed in reincarnation, I would say I once lived as a cat."

Ginger couldn't help but smile. Professor Moody did have a certain look of an overfed, bemused feline about him.

"Willington taught here at the Institute from time to time. His work was connected with the new field of Quantum Physics, which in my opinion is still far too new a field to be placing much weight on. Anyway, I think he was fishing for an invitation to present his work to our students after he had successfully tested it. He hinted that I should use my influence to secure the invitation."

"Were you inclined to do so?" Ginger asked.

Professor Moody snorted. "Not on the subject of time travel. That's all codswallop."

"Have you studied his calculations? To determine that his claims are unfounded?"

"I haven't had the opportunity. Willington is extremely secretive."

"That's interesting," Ginger said. "When my son and I visited his booth at the Inventions and Innovations Exhibition, he allowed me to take a photograph of his design and calculations before he wiped the blackboard clean."

Shock flashed through Rupert Moody's eyes. "He let you see his calculations?"

"Well, he showed us something," Ginger said. "I couldn't really tell you if they were actual or fictional."

"He's been known to write down small fragments of his calculations in public," Professor Willington said, "perhaps a diagram or two. Nothing specific though. He has a patent pending."

"He told us that it was the entire sum of calculations. He wanted my son, Scout, to see it."

"Your son, is he a gifted student of physics?"

"He's a bright boy with a quick mind," Ginger stated proudly. "Professor Willington seemed quite taken with him. But, no, Scout is showing more interest in equine husbandry."

The professor's mouth seemed to be working hard, as if this information was hard to digest. "You say you took a photograph?" he said, finally.

"Yes."

"I, er . . . don't suppose I could have a look at that photograph."

"For what purpose, since you think it's all 'codswallop'?"

"Purely for academic entertainment. I think my colleagues and I would like to have a good laugh." He smiled, a nervous sort of smile. "You've had the photograph developed, haven't you?" Professor Moody's eyes flashed with concern. "It's not still on your camera, is it? Something could happen to the film. You could drop it by mistake."

"I have my own darkroom at my office, Professor Moody. I can assure you the film has been developed and the photograph is quite safe. However, Professor Willington was very clear that we were not to show it to anyone."

"Of course, of course." Professor Moody waved a fleshy hand.

"Do you have any idea where Professor Willington has gone?" Ginger asked.

"I'm afraid I have no idea, Mrs. Reed."

"Did Professor Willington ever mention concerns for his safety? Perhaps a feeling that he was being followed?"

"You mean the government man?"

Ginger tilted her head in question. "Government man?"

"Yes, Willington told me on more than one occasion that he thought he was being stalked by a mysterious figure. Willington is always spouting one kind of conspiracy theory or another. He was sure he was being watched by British intelligence or something. I don't know."

"Why on earth would the British government be shadowing an eccentric professor?" Ginger asked.

"That's a good question," Professor Moody said with a shrug.

4

Ginger sat down on a bench in the north end of St. James Park where Magna was already waiting. The day was pleasantly warm, and Magna had suggested earlier that they meet there instead of at the office. Nearby people bought ice cream at a stand, families sat on tartan blankets picnicking, couples strolled by holding hands, and children played a raucous game of catch.

"They did have someone watching the professor," Magna said, forgoing any pleasantries as was her style.

"Is that so?" Ginger said, no longer surprised at how adept Magna was at gathering information.

Magna gave a tight nod. "I searched the professor's laboratory this morning as you requested. What an interesting mess!"

"I'm sorry I missed seeing it," Ginger said, her curiosity piqued.

"Oh, you'd love it," Magna returned with a sly grin. "It has some very bright lighting and smells like oil and metal. The walls are lined with shelves and cabinets filled with all sorts of books and tools and gadgets. There are workbenches sat willy-nilly, covered with what I can only surmise are half-finished inventions. Gears and cogs and pulleys strewn across the floor, coils of wire . . . I thought I had entered into the world of Jules Verne or something."

Ginger hummed. "Any signs of an explosion?"

"If a bomb had gone off in there, it might not look any different than it does now. But no, I didn't find any scorch marks or signs of recent shock."

"Was the time travel suit I described on the premises?"

"It was not."

"Diagrams of any kind? Drawings?"

Magna cocked her head. "That was the odd thing. In all of that chaos, I didn't find a single diagram or plan."

"I believe Professor Willington held those things

closer to his chest," Ginger said. "Now why would the British government have a man watching the professor?"

"According to my source, the professor was working on new types of explosive devices but had not turned over the details to the military. Apparently, the agency fears Willington might sell the plans to certain foreign governments. When he was approached by the Crown to divulge what he had, he refused. They didn't have enough evidence gathered at that stage to arrest him, so they assigned someone from MI5 to monitor him."

"Oh mercy," Ginger said with a sigh. MI5, or Military Intelligence Section 5, would be interested in a man with an above-average IQ who made spectacular scientific claims. "I wonder, has Professor Willington been abducted?"

"By his own government?"

"Either that, or by foreign government agents."

"That doesn't explain the note left for his housekeeper," Magna said.

"Perhaps he wrote it before he was captured. I don't doubt that he believed his time machine would work. He could have written the note, arranged for it to be delivered by courier, and then had his plans derailed."

"What about your other theory?" Magna's dark brow arched. "Your Professor Moody kidnaps him."

"It's just that, a theory."

Magna slowly waved her arm in a straight line in front of herself, saying dramatically. "*Jealous inventor kidnaps a rival and holds him as prisoner until time travel secrets are revealed.* You have to admit that would make a great headline."

"Really, Magna. Sometimes I think you read too many adventure novels."

"I do love a ripping adventure yarn," Magna conceded. "Speaking of which, I did check with the ticketing agencies as you suggested. Edward Willington boarded a ship to Marseilles just two days after you saw him. From there he went to Algiers. He was there for two days and then came back on the same route."

"He actually went to get his mythical Kronium," Ginger said with a note of amazement. "I hadn't heard about such a substance, so I contacted the University of London's Department of Geology and Mineralogy and also King's College. When they couldn't tell me anything, I checked with the Royal Mineralogical Society."

"And?"

"Apparently it's like the yeti—some people think

it exists, but no one has any proof. It's believed to have almost magical qualities. Professor Willington said he had only recently confirmed its existence."

"More likely that he believed the words of some unscrupulous confidence man in Algiers who claimed to own a mining company," Magna said with mild derision, "and made that long trip only to be duped in the end."

"Presumably your contact at MI5 didn't say if the government might be holding Professor Willington?" Ginger asked.

"Since holding a man against his will without due cause is illegal, that kind of information would be well guarded and beyond the scope of what my source could tell me. Do you think Basil might know something? Perhaps Scotland Yard has made a discovery."

"Basil hasn't mentioned anything. He's not usually brought into such matters unless a murder is involved, and I certainly hope that's not the case with Professor Willington."

"If the British government is holding the professor, we can't do much about it, and if a foreign government has kidnapped him, we can't do much about that either," Magna said. "Are we at an impasse?"

"Perhaps," Ginger conceded. "But I want to continue our quest to find him until we know for sure. I think I'll make a trip to Fernleigh House in the morning. I know you've just been, but you're welcome to join me."

"Are you driving?" Magna said mischievously. "Then I'm coming!"

5

After Mrs. Rawlings had let them in the next day at Fernleigh House, Ginger found the laboratory to be in the very condition Magna had described. With gloved hands she fished through the professor's desk drawers, finding nothing of merit aside from a collection of pencil stubs, scraps of paper with unintelligible scribblings, and the odd invoice for general supplies.

"It does look like a small tornado has passed through here," Ginger said as she perused the tops of the workbenches and eyed the debris on the floor. She made sure to examine everything, as sometimes the smallest, seemingly insignificant item turned out to be the key to unlock the case, but in this instance, nothing caught her eye.

She placed her hand on her hip, feeling the satiny fabric of her day frock—a pink number patterned with delicately embroidered rose petals, an asymmetrical collar, and a handkerchief hemline —and let out a long breath. Trees blowing outside the window caught her eye and she stepped closer, peering out. "What's that?" she said, pointing.

In the distance behind an overgrown grove was something that looked like a wooden roof top.

"A shed?" Magna offered as she stepped alongside her.

"Shall we have a look?" Ginger asked, already walking towards the laboratory doorway.

The wooden structure had once been painted white but had weathered grey, leaving only hints of its former colour. The rusted hinges on the old doors creaked loudly in protest as Ginger pulled them open. A waft of must and mildew greeted them.

Parked inside was an old delivery van with the word *Leyland* written on the bonnet. Rust had claimed much of the metal that showed hints of green. The registration plates on it were so corroded that one couldn't read half of the numbers.

"That's been sitting here for a while," Magna said.

The cement floor of the shed was covered in

dust. Light came in through small windows, the corners of which were quite clearly home to an array of spiders. All manner of gears, springs, screws and wires were scattered haphazardly along a workbench, and rusted hammers and saws hung from equally rusted nails on the walls.

"The gardener keeps his tools in another shed nearer to the house," Magna offered, "and is far more meticulous than the owner of this one."

"I'm not even sure what we're looking for," Ginger said. "Perhaps some kind of a gadget related to weaponry or something. Something that would indicate he was working on something MI5 would be interested in."

"Would we even know what that looked like if we found it?"

Ginger's gazed landed on a scuff mark in the dust by the workbench. Bending down, she started removing some of the contents on the bottom shelf beneath the bench.

"What are you looking for?"

"The dust has been stirred up here. I thought perhaps . . ." Ginger grabbed the heaviest-looking object, which looked like some kind of very banged-up toolbox, only to discover it was lighter than it looked. "Empty," she said as she pulled it out. "Curious. Oh, wait." Under where the empty box had been sitting was what looked like a hidden trapdoor. She tugged on a piece of twine, opening the door. "There's a compartment built underneath the cement floor. Hand me your torch."

Magna handed over the small torch she kept in her trouser pocket and Ginger shone the light beam into the compartment.

"There's a metal box inside," Ginger said, "about the size of a small suitcase." She tugged on the handle, pulling it out. It was locked with a heavy padlock.

Standing, Ginger brushed the dust off the knees of her stockings and straightened her frock.

"We must open it," Magna said.

"It's private property," Ginger replied weakly. Considering they'd already broken into the shed, which was also private property, her protest didn't really hold water.

Magna shot Ginger a look. "The professor is not here, Ginger, he's in the year 2028."

"Righto. Well, let's get to it, then."

Ginger and Magna lifted the heavily constructed case onto the workbench after Magna had cleared a spot.

"The lock doesn't seem to want to open," Ginger

said after trying out various tools from her lock-picking kit."

"Sometimes older locks are hard to open like that," Magna offered.

Ginger quickly found a heavy steel mallet and held it aloft with gloved hands. She brought the hammer down, completely missing the lock and delivering a glancing blow to the side of the case.

"Certainly a creative approach," Magna quipped.

Ginger blew a lock of red hair out of her face and lifted the heavy mallet again.

"Wait!" Magna said as she walked over to the van, opened the passenger door, and looked in the glovebox. A moment later she held up a key.

"Surely that won't work," Ginger said. "You think he would hide the key in the glovebox?"

"That's where I would have put it," Magna said as she handed over the key. "Remember we are dealing with a very cagey mind."

Ginger slipped the key into the padlock and instantly there was a click.

"Cagey mind, indeed," she said.

Inside the box they found an envelope and a set of number plates for a vehicle, along with a set of keys. Inside the envelope was a deed.

"This is an address for a property out near

Luton," Ginger said, reading the official-looking document.

"Luton? What is Luton?" Magna wasn't from Britain and not as familiar with all the towns.

"It's in Bedfordshire."

Ginger held up the deed. "It doesn't mention a house, just a property,"

Magna grabbed the keys and the plates. Both women turned to look at the old van.

"You don't suppose . . ." Magna said.

Ginger opened the driver's side door as the hinges groaned mightily. The key was inserted into the ignition easily. The engine coughed to life, settling into a rough idle.

"Purrs like a cat," Ginger said.

"More like a cat with indigestion."

"I'll wager those are fake number plates in the case. It looks to me like he wanted this vehicle to be completely off any official records." She grinned at Magna. "Care to join me on a journey north?"

"Not in that thing," Magna said.

6

Ginger's white 1924 Crossley sports touring convertible was her pride and joy, at least when it came to mechanical things. The weather was warm enough to ride with the top down. She tied a silk scarf over her head, knotting it under her chin. Glancing at her passenger, she said, "Would you like one? There's an extra scarf in the glovebox."

Magna shook her head. "I prefer to feel the wind blow."

To each their own, Ginger thought as she pulled onto the tarmacked surface of the carriageway and directed her motorcar north. A man driving a black Ford honked his horn vigorously just as Ginger pulled onto the road and swerved to avoid hitting the rear end of the Crossley. He waved his arm in the air and seemed to be shouting something.

"What's he on about?" Ginger said, staring at the reflection of the disgruntled man in the rear-view mirror.

Magna's smile pulled at the corner of her lips. "I believe he thinks you pulled out in front of him, cutting him off."

"Some people just seem to be in a hurry all the time," Ginger said with some irony as her foot stomped on the accelerator of her sports tourer. The six-cylinder engine responded nicely by shooting the vehicle forward like a horse lunging into the race. In only a moment the Ford seemed like a small toy as it receded quickly in the mirror.

"Tally-ho!" Ginger laughed as she squeezed the rubber ball of the brass horn, honking it.

"Let's go!" Magna cried, lifting a fist into the air, as the green fields, pasturelands and villages flew by in a blur.

"You know you always seem happy to drive with me," Ginger said thoughtfully. "Strangely, I can't say that about anyone else."

"You know me," Magna said with an amused glance in Ginger's direction. "I love a good bit of grave danger mixed with an afternoon of sunshine."

"Pfft, this isn't dangerous," Ginger scoffed, then added seriously, "Oh bother, I seem to be in need of petrol." She stared down at a glowing orange light mounted just below the dashboard, which she had had installed so she wouldn't have to read the fuel dipstick.

"Ah, we're in luck," Magna said. "There's a garage ahead."

Ginger swerved into the opposite side of the road to pass a Bentley.

"Some people slow down when pulling off a road," Magna said.

"Indeed," Ginger said, easing up on the accelerator as she pulled off the road, the Bentley going past with the driver sounding his horn and yelling something incomprehensible.

The establishment was called "Lawrence's Garage," and fortunately Lawrence, whoever he was, had the good sense to have a few barrels of petrol available for those who, like Ginger, had forgotten to fill their tanks before heading off into the country. The ladies got out of the car and stepped away to avoid the awful fumes.

"Don't look right away," Ginger said, "but do you see that blue Austin behind us, parked under those trees?"

Magna pretended to watch birds in the sky, turning slowly in a circle as she did. "I do."

"I believe he's been following us at quite a distance since we left Fernleigh House, and now he's pulled over."

Magna took another quick glance, careful not to look like she was staring. "Are we being followed?" she said, sounding just a little bit excited.

"I'm going to leave the carriageway at my first opportunity and see if he follows us down a side route."

"I wonder if he's from MI5?" Magna said.

Ginger chuckled. "Whoever he is, he's about to learn that a woman can drive just as well as any man."

Magna laughed, and at Ginger's questioning look, began to cough. "Forgive me, it's just rather ironic, isn't it? You and me being followed by British intelligence. 'Two former spies go rogue.' What a great novel that would make!"

"And we thought we had finished with that lot," Ginger said. "They learned somehow that we were investigating the professor's disappearance and have probably been tracking us for longer than we'd like to think."

"Perhaps they suspect that we are harbouring him and want to keep us under observation."

"Let's see if we can make the job a little bit harder than they bargained for." Ginger paid for the petrol. Once she and Magna were seated, she forcefully slammed the Crossley into gear and stomped on the accelerator.

The vehicle responded to the weight of Ginger's foot and careened onto the road. Ginger glanced into the mirror and saw the Austin pull onto the tarmacked surface.

With the Crossley's engine roaring, Ginger drove now at an even faster pace, passing several cars almost as if they were standing still.

"Woo ha! *Très bien!*" Magna shouted as Ginger passed a slow-moving lorry on a blind corner, pulling onto the gravelly edge of the road. Stones flew from the rear wheels as she honked her horn.

The burly-looking lorry driver raised a fist. "Bloody 'ell!"

"I don't see why he's upset," Ginger shouted. "How else can one pass safely on a blind corner!"

With a chirp of the wheels, the motorcar bounced back onto the smooth asphalt. It took a few minutes, but the Austin she'd been trying to dodge passed the lorry and re-emerged in Ginger's line of sight.

"Here we go," Ginger said, as the Crossley slowed down just enough to make a left turn onto a farm track heading north. The Austin did the same.

"He's definitely following us," Magna said.

The Crossley rattled and shook terribly on the rough, narrow track as Ginger travelled as fast as she could past the fields and hedges. She managed to keep the Austin at a distance as it struggled over the bumpy surface.

They came over a rise and encountered a slow-moving horse-drawn hay wagon, forcing Ginger to apply the brakes mightily. Magna braced herself with one arm against the dashboard.

"I don't fancy being buried in hay today, do you?" Ginger said as the car slowed to a snail's pace. A rough stone wall about six feet high bordered one side of the road and on the other was a drainage ditch, making it impossible to pass the hay wagon.

Abruptly, the hay wagon turned right through a break in the wall that served as an access into the field beyond.

"Hold on!" Ginger cranked the steering wheel, driving the Crossley through the same break in the wall stopping along the wall out of view of the road.

In short order the rumble of the Austin reached them, then gradually quieted as it drove by.

"It's like we have our own time machine," Ginger said. "He'll think we've disappeared into thin air."

"Well played, Mrs. Reed," Magna said. She sighed happily as she leaned back in her seat. "I'm having a wonderful afternoon."

7

The address on the deed took them to a small property about three miles east of the town of Luton. A humble stone wall bordered the front of the property, and Ginger turned onto the rutted driveway that led to a small stone cottage covered in climbing ivy. Nestled in a grove of tall oak trees, the house remained out of the sight of the road. A steeply sloped thatched roof had two rounded windows looking out from the front of the cottage like sleepy eyes. The whole thing looked like something out of a storybook.

"Are we going to encounter seven little fellows with long beards, carrying mining tools?" Magna asked as they climbed out of the Crossley.

Ginger bent over to examine a set of tracks in the

driveway. "That's the same tread pattern belonging to that van we found at Fernleigh."

After receiving no answer at the door, Magna reached out for the thumb latch on the iron door handle. "Locked."

Walking to the back of the house, they found a large open space with more of the same style of tyre tracks. Two parallel ruts worn out in the earth led off into the woods.

"He's been back here with that van many times," Ginger said, gesturing towards the trees.

They found the back door locked as well.

"I hear a cat in distress, don't you?" Ginger said.

Magna rolled her eyes. "Perhaps the cat is a cousin to Miss Fluffington. Perhaps its name is *Miss Trespassington*."

"Very funny." Ginger removed her lock picks from her handbag. It took only a moment to manipulate the old lock.

"Hello," she called out as the door swung open. "Anyone home?"

The cottage was cosy and compact with low ceilings, exposed wooden beams, and a large stone fireplace. A small kitchen had a wood-burning stove. The furniture was rustic but seemed to be in good shape. One framed picture of the professor hung on the wall. He was posing with what must have been two of his students, the three of them standing in front of the main entrance of the Kelvin Institute.

"That picture is proof that this cottage is occupied by the professor," Ginger said.

Magna opened a door. "The bedroom."

Ginger followed her inside the cramped room. Along with a narrow bed and a wooden wardrobe, it contained a workbench with a full array of tools.

"He liked to sleep with his projects," Magna said.

On the bench Ginger found several schematic drawings. One had sketches of what appeared to be a helium balloon, similar to the elongated balloons she'd seen during the Great War, which were used to observe enemy troops. This one, though, had several modifications, and, according to the notes written on the sketches, could be filled with helium and launched by only one operator.

Magna pointed to the sketches. "It notes that the balloon was designed for long-distance flight and has a built-in petrol motor operating a propeller."

Ginger found some more diagrams of various devices such as something called an "Advanced Superheterodyne Radio Receiver" and other assorted electronic and mechanical devices.

"This is interesting," Magna said, picking up a

plan that was lying on another workbench. "It looks like some kind of small explosive device."

"That could be what MI5 is after," Ginger said. "Looks like a grenade of some kind."

"He's labelled it 'Flash Grenade'," Magna noted.

Ginger took a closer look at the notes. "It says it has almost no concussive force and can be set with a timer. It is designed for theatre and gives off only a small noise but emits a very bright flash of light."

Ginger and Magna shared a look.

"Theatre indeed," Magna said, "like the play about the inventor who fakes his own disappearance."

"Very clever," Ginger said.

Magna found a shoebox containing three letters under the bed. "The postmarks say they are all from the town of Ramsey."

"I think that's on the Isle of Man."

"How odd," Magna said.

Ginger put them in order according to the dates on the postmark, sat on the bed, and began to read the oldest one aloud.

My dear Edward,

How delightful to hear from you after all these years. I'm surprised you found me! I'm pleased to hear you are alive and well and, from the sound of it, furiously productive as you always were. Some called you eccentric, but I always thought of you as brilliantly unorthodox in ways that were very endearing to me.

Thank you for your condolences. My Fred was a good man who gave me a good life. His passing away, now ten years ago, was unexpected. Unfortunately, we were not able to have children, but I have been blessed with some very good friends here in Ramsey, and they surround me with care and support.

To answer your question, of course I remember the romance we had when we were young and both living in London. That was a very sweet time and I thank you for reminding me of it. I have a fond memory of our time at your parents' cottage in Luton, when you first kissed me, out in the woods. I wonder if the oak with our names carved on it is still standing. Of course, one can wonder what would have happened if I had stayed in England instead of moving here with my parents. But I was only sixteen, in many ways just a girl really, and not ready to strike out on my own despite the pleadings of one very handsome young inventor.

Thank you for your concern over my health. I am in some pain, but it is manageable for now. The doctors say I have about a year, but who really knows?

Please let's keep writing. I would love to hear more about your latest inventions.

Yours,

Elizabeth Chatwood

Ginger picked up the next one which was dated three weeks after the first.

Dear Edward,

A time machine! Of course, you would be the one to invent that. How wonderful!

Do you plan on using it to go back in time to those few months in London that we shared together? What a lark! It's fun to think about what might have been, isn't it?

It is so interesting to hear about your teaching experiences at the Kelvin Institute. I can easily imagine you standing in front of all those bright young people. I bet they enjoyed you tremendously. Even when you were a lad of sixteen, you were very generous with your knowledge and had a knack for communicating your ideas. I remember your sketches for what you called the 'Relaxation Hat'. Something that massaged your scalp while you went about your day. Do you remember? I'm sorry I laughed at your drawings, but you must admit they were humorous.

You'll have to forgive me for the short letters, my strength does fail me sometimes. But please keep writing, I am enjoying your correspondence very much!

Yours,

Elizabeth

P.S. Your plan to travel to the future to find a cure for my cancer sounds like something from a novel. How romantic! Your earnestness made me smile. I want you to know that I heartily endorse the plan and will be eagerly awaiting your arrival with the cure!

The last one was dated a week before the professor's disappearance.

Dear Edward,

I'm so sorry to hear that your time machine did not work. It would have been grand fun, wouldn't it?

Yes, of course I would love to see you again! How exciting. I'm not sure you'll recognize me, and I hope you won't be too alarmed at my aged and frail appearance. Fred built a guest house in the garden, and you can stay as long as you like. My staff will take good care of you. Our cook makes the best bangers and mash (I remember you loved that).

There are several steamship lines that come to Douglas Harbour. I am not sure what you meant by

*'floating right to my front door on prevailing winds',
but it gave me a chuckle nonetheless. I shall be
watching the next easterlies for any sign of you.*

Yours,

Elizabeth

"I think the mystery is solving itself," Magna said.

"Shall we check out the tracks leading into the woods?" Ginger asked as she got to her feet.

"Lead the way."

The tracks took them to a clearing with all the evidence to the professor's disappearance in place: ropes, unwound and threading through the grass, and a petrol-powered compressor that showed signs of rust.

"Tent pegs," Magna said, toeing one with her shoe.

"If one didn't know better," Ginger added, "one would think the debris had been discarded by vagrants." She looked to the sky. "And not by an adventurous inventor making a grand gesture for someone he loves."

8

"It's the first time I have ever seen Magna's eyes well up," Ginger told Basil the next evening as they sipped a brandy, sharing the settee in the sitting room.

"Good heavens." Basil's eyebrows shot up. "You mean she has a soft spot?"

"Well, she tried to hide it, but she was dabbing at her eyes when we found their initials etched into a big oak out in the woods," Ginger said warmly. "She also snatched up all the letters and diagrams from the cottage before we left. She said she couldn't stand the thought of MI5 finding them."

"You couldn't stop her?"

"I didn't try."

"Private property, you know."

"You'll have to arrest her then."

"Hmph," Basil said, rolling his eyes.

"She'll give them back to Professor Willington if he ever turns up again," Ginger remarked.

"And how did you gain access to the cottage?" Basil said, "Let me guess. You heard a cat in distress."

Ginger started to speak but thought better of it.

"Do you really think the British secret service is after the professor?" Basil asked.

"Someone is." Ginger stared at the red embers in the hearth. "It seems entirely plausible to me. He was working on all sorts of things the government would be interested in."

"And what about the van? You said there were fake number plates, didn't you?"

"I assume so," Ginger answered. "I think he wanted to remain off any official records with his activities and used his cottage in Luton to attempt to do so, transporting materials pertaining to his inventions over a period of time."

Basil nodded. "I would think it would have been a very perilous journey, from Luton to the Isle of Man in a balloon."

"I consulted John Spellings," Ginger said casually.

Basil ducked his chin, turning to eye Ginger with interest. "The famous hot air balloon pilot?"

"The same," Ginger said. "In fact, he and Professor Willington worked together on a propulsion system for balloons years ago." Ginger stretched out her legs, then curled them under again. "He told me the journey would be challenging and dangerous, but he felt that the professor was capable of navigating a balloon that distance. It would have taken about twenty-eight hours in his estimation."

Basil offered an appreciative whistle.

Ginger grinned. "I can easily picture the professor, up in that balloon, goggles strapped on, his wild hair whipping in the wind."

"Hmm, quite," Basil said. "So, the case is closed then. What will you tell the lady who hired you?"

"I consider it closed. I have no wish to bother the professor. I will simply tell Mrs. Rawlings that we found nothing." Ginger snuggled in under Basil's arm. "Sometimes cases go unsolved. It's possible the professor will turn up here again, just as magically as he left."

That day might come, Ginger thought, but not until his dear Elizabeth was gone from this earth. Ginger was happy the two romantics would have a second chance at love, even if it came late and short. Love finds a way.

If you enjoyed reading *Lady Gold Investigates Vol 6* please help others enjoy it too.

Recommend it: Help others find the book by recommending it to friends, readers' groups, discussion boards and by **suggesting it to your local library.**

Review it: Please tell other readers why you liked this book by reviewing it at leestrauss-books.com

* No spoilers please *

Don't miss the next Ginger Gold mystery~
MURDER AT MADAME TUSSAUDS

Family secrets are murder!

When Ginger's former sister-in-law Felicia, now Lady Davenport-Witt, first received a mysterious note in the post, she dismissed it as coming from a nuisance writer. These things were known to happen to those who enjoyed social popularity. But with a third one, she began to feel ill at ease.

Ginger, however, had been worried since the first short missive had arrived. Someone knew of a family secret that would upset Felicia's apple cart in a very big way.

Felicia's new hobby of photography turned into freelance work for a London paper, and her first assignment was to attend the wedding of the new Duke of Worthington and his very young bride-to-be taking place at St. Paul's Cathedral. Murder follows matrimony, and Felicia finds herself in the middle of the muddle.

Can Ginger help Felicia navigate the twists and turns of fate and stop a second death?

Shop at leestraussbooks.com

GINGER GOLD'S JOURNAL

Did you know that Ginger kept a Journal?

Sign up for Lee's readers list and gain access to **Ginger Gold's private Journal.** Find out about Ginger's Life before the SS *Rosa* and how she became the woman she has. This is a fluid document that will cover her romance with her late husband Daniel, her time serving in the British secret service during World War One, and beyond. Includes a recipe for Dark Dutch Chocolate Cake!

It begins: **July 31, 1912**

How fabulous that I found this Journal today, hidden in the bottom of my wardrobe. Good old Pippins, our English butler in London, gave it to me as a parting gift when Father whisked me away on our American adventure so he could marry Sally. Pips said it was for me to record my new adventures. I'm ashamed I never even penned one word before today. I think I was just too sad.

This old leather-bound journal takes me back to that emotional time. I had shed enough tears to fill the ocean and I remember telling

Father dramatically that I was certain to cause flooding to match God's. At eight years old I was well-trained in my biblical studies, though, in retro-spect, I would say that I had probably bordered on heresy with my little tantrum.

The first week of my "adventure" was spent with a tummy ache and a number of embarrassing sessions that involved a bucket and Father holding back my long hair so I wouldn't soil it with vomit.

I certainly felt that I was being punished for some reason. Hartigan House—though large and sometimes lonely—was my home and Pips was my good friend. He often helped me to pass the time with games of I Spy and Xs and Os.

"Very good, Little Miss," he'd say with a twinkle in his blue eyes when I won, which I did often. I suspect now that our good butler wasn't beyond letting me win even when unmerited.

Father had got it into his silly head that I needed a mother, but I think the truth was he wanted a wife. Sally, a woman half my father's age, turned out to be a sufficient wife in the end, but I could never claim her as a mother.

Well, Pips, I'm sure you'd be happy to know that things turned out all right here in America.

SUBSCRIBE to read more!
http://www.leestraussbooks.com/
gingergoldjournalsignup/

MORE FROM LEE STRAUSS

Shop at leestraussbooks.com

GINGER GOLD MYSTERY SERIES (cozy 1920s historical)

Cozy. Charming. Filled with Bright Young Things. This Jazz Age murder mystery will entertain and delight you with its 1920s flair and pizzazz!

Murder on the SS Rosa

Murder at Hartigan House

Murder at Bray Manor

Murder at Feathers & Flair

Murder at the Mortuary

Murder at Kensington Gardens

Murder at St. George's Church

The Wedding of Ginger & Basil

Murder Aboard the Flying Scotsman

Murder at the Boat Club

Murder on Eaton Square

Murder by Plum Pudding

Murder on Fleet Street

Murder at Brighton Beach

Murder in Hyde Park

Murder at the Royal Albert Hall

Murder in Belgravia

Murder on Mallowan Court

Murder at the Savoy

Murder at the Circus

Murder in France

Murder at Yuletide

Murder at Madame Tussauds

Murder at St. Paul's Cathedral

LADY GOLD INVESTIGATES (Ginger Gold companion short stories)

Volume 1

Volume 2

Volume 3

Volume 4

Volume 5

HIGGINS & HAWKE MYSTERY SERIES (cozy 1930s

Marlow finds himself teamed up with intelligent and savvy Sage Farrell, a girl so far out of his league he feels blinded in her presence - literally - damned glasses! Together they work to find the identity of @gingerbreadman. Can they stop the killer before he strikes again?

Gingerbread Man

Life Is but a Dream

Hickory Dickory Dock

Twinkle Little Star

LIGHT & LOVE (sweet romance)

Set in the dazzling charm of Europe, follow Katja, Gabriella, Eva, Anna and Belle as they find strength, hope and love.

Love Song

Your Love is Sweet

In Light of Us

Lying in Starlight

PLAYING WITH MATCHES (WW2 history/romance)

A sobering but hopeful journey about how one young German boy copes with the war and propaganda. Based on true events.

A Piece of Blue String (companion short story)

THE CLOCKWISE COLLECTION (YA time travel romance)

Casey Donovan has issues: hair, height and uncontrollable trips to the 19th century! And now this ~ she's accidentally taken Nate Mackenzie, the cutest boy in the school, back in time. Awkward.

Clockwise

Clockwiser

Like Clockwork

Counter Clockwise

Clockwork Crazy

Clocked (companion novella)

<u>Standalones</u>

Seaweed

Love, Tink

ABOUT THE AUTHORS

Lee Strauss is a USA TODAY bestselling author of The Ginger Gold Mysteries series, The Higgins & Hawke Mystery series, The Rosa Reed Mystery series (cozy historical mysteries), A Nursery Rhyme Mystery series (mystery suspense), The Perception series (young adult dystopian), The Light & Love series (sweet romance), The Clockwise Collection (YA time travel romance), and young adult historical fiction with over a million books read. She has titles published in German, Spanish and Korean, and a growing audio library.

When Lee's not writing or reading she likes to cycle, hike, and stare at the ocean. She loves to drink caffè lattes and red wines in exotic places, and eat dark chocolate anywhere.

For more info on books by Lee Strauss and her social media links, visit leestraussbooks.com. To make sure you don't miss the next new release, be sure to sign up for her readers' list!

Norm Strauss is a singer-songwriter and performing artist who's seen the stage of The Voice of Germany. Short story writing is a new passion he shares with his wife Lee Strauss. Find out more at norm@norm-strauss.com

www.leestraussbooks.com
leestraussbooks@gmail.com